THE MARTELLO
TOWER

THE MARTELLO TOWER

William Haggard

Hodder & Stoughton
LONDON SYDNEY AUCKLAND TORONTO

British Library Cataloguing in Publication Data
Haggard, William
  The martello tower.
  Rn: Richard Henry Michael Clayton
  I. Title
  823'.914[F]   PR6053.L38

  ISBN 0-340-39213-4

Hodder and Stoughton Editorial Office: 47 Bedford Square, London WC1B 3DP.

THE MARTELLO
TOWER

1

Arthur Tribe threw the local newspaper on the floor in a fury. A woman had been mugged in the sedate market town and had been taken to the neighbourhood hospital. She had been savaged but was reported stable. Whatever that idiotic word meant.

His world was falling to pieces about his ears.

Moreover he had once known her well. He too had been in hospital after a lorry racing to catch a ship had pushed him off the Dover road. Janet Clegg had been a senior nurse and had cared for him with a cool professionalism which he had valued far more than an overt sympathy. She had been a quiet woman, too, which had pleased him. They had got on a good deal better than well and twice he had nearly asked her to marry him for she was unpaired and he a widower. But the memory of a previous marriage had stopped him in his tracks like a stone, the ceaseless clatter of a shrew's sharp tongue.

Nevertheless he had known regret and something which was close to self-contempt. This might be the conventional wisdom but in a very real sense it was also cowardice. It was playing it safe which was no doubt admirable but without a stake on the table you couldn't win. Janet might have brought him a big one and she had signalled she might be willing to give it a run.

But he was well enough as he was, alone. He cooked for himself and a woman cleaned weekly; he had a modest but not beggarly pension; he liked to walk and his dog liked it better; he smoked and drank in moderation and had a hi-fi on which he played jazz and string quartets. He knew that Janet had retired in her turn and occasionally he saw her shopping in the high street of the neighbouring market

7

town. He knew where she lived but had never called for that would have struck him as most unseemly. Once he had decided against re-marriage it would have been unseemly to have presumed on a professional relationship. Unseemly was one of his two favourite words. The other was fair, what was just and decent.

He was a very English Englishman, set in his ways and in no way ashamed of them.

And now though he wouldn't see her still he must contact her when she came out of hospital. For there was something he must do for Janet Clegg.

He put on the hi-fi, mixed a drink and reflected. What had happened to Janet was grossly unfair – probably some drop-out from Gleaville down from London on a cheap day ticket and after money for some horrible drug. He had found that ugly resort too crowded and had drifted across to the market town.

Where he had struck down a middle-aged woman brutally, kicking her as she lay in the gutter, taking her bag and the few pounds in it. A few pounds but a whole week's money for shopping. An elderly man had tried to stop him and got a knee in his groin for his pains in doing so.

That simply wasn't right or seemly. It had happened once and could happen again.

But not to Janet Clegg, it shouldn't. He, Arthur Tribe, must see to that.

He had fought in a war and been treated fairly. That had impressed him since he hadn't expected it. His platoon sergeant had been an Irishman and Arthur had made some remark about Ireland. Promptly his life had become a misery or had until a young Major had learnt of it and had had him transferred to another company. That had been an act of justice. Arthur Tribe had forgotten the Major's name but after the war he had left the army. Tribe had heard that he'd gone into something secret where he'd risen to the top with aplomb. Well, whatever it was he would do it competently; he'd had a streak of almost total ruthlessness but would never do anything he himself deemed unworthy.

Such as savaging a defenceless woman.

Tribe picked up the paper but threw it down again. He felt physically sick but not frustrated for there was something he could do and would. He too had left the army after the war, joining the Prison Service contentedly. He had risen to be a governor, though not of a famous or infamous prison. His private ethos ran against such promotion since it wasn't in the now fashionable stream. Judges sent men to prison for punishment, not primarily for reform or brainwash. That wasn't in line with current thinking and Arthur Tribe was a simple man who couldn't have concealed his opinions even if he'd thought it proper to do so.

But of course whichever prison they gave one it must be run with an unflinching fairness. Clever lawyers talked about natural justice, a phrase which Arthur Tribe mistrusted, but fairness was something concrete, quotidian.

That affair of Harry Wellworthy, for instance. It was a parallel, Tribe remembered smiling, to what had happened to himself in the army. Wellworthy had been a small-time criminal, in prison not for some famous crime but for a series of petty thefts and swindles; and there had fallen foul of the Cypriot Marcos who, as a criminal of major standing, shouldn't have been in Tribe's prison at all. Unlike Arthur Tribe in his days in the army Wellworthy had said nothing offensive but Marcos had taken against him relentlessly; he had resented his speech and his air of gentility and had taken it out in the dozen ways by which a big man in prison could bully a small. When Arthur Tribe had discovered this he had asked for Marco's transfer at once. That had been only fair and seemly. The request had done him no good professionally but he had known too much about life in his Service to suppose that he or his overworked staff could stamp out persistent, organised bullying by one of the prison's respected barons. At the time Harry Wellworthy had been ardently grateful and Tribe wondered if he

9

remained so still. Sufficiently grateful to do him a favour even if that meant breaking the law again.

It was the morning for his cleaning woman and he made her a cup of tea as she came in. She could have made it for herself just as well but the gesture was a formal ritual, establishing their relationship firmly. He paid her money but she wasn't his drudge. She was a shrewd, well-read woman who liked to talk. The women of her own circle bored her and she cleaned for Tribe and two others like him as much for the chance of intelligent chatter (she didn't stop work as she talked her head off) as for the money she earned by doing the chores.

This morning she was full of Janet Clegg. "You've seen the paper, of course?"

"It made me sick."

"It put me on the boil, I can tell you. It should never have happened."

"Then how to stop it?"

"That Janet Clegg should have carried a pistol."

He was startled and didn't attempt to hide it. The thought was sufficiently close to his own to be something more than a pointless coincidence. If there were others who seemed to think as he did then, though he'd be breaking the law, perhaps that law was just as silly as he, Arthur Tribe, thought it badly administered. He began to probe.

"She wouldn't have got a licence – not a hope."

"But you've got a gun all right. It's unfair."

The word wounded him and he tried to explain. "I've got a licence for a sporting shotgun since I've also permission to shoot on the saltings. It lives in a case in a couple of pieces. If anyone came in and attacked me it would take me thirty seconds at least to put it together, then load and fire. Quite useless against a determined thief."

She was mollified but pursued him relentlessly. "Why don't you keep it ready, loaded?"

"Because I was taught that that was dangerous. In any case it would make no odds. I couldn't sleep with it in my bed like a wife; I'd still have to get to wherever I kept it and by that time I'd have been coshed unconscious."

"What would happen if you tried for a pistol?"

"I'd have no more hope than did Janet Clegg."

She exploded in sudden and genuine anger. "The law is an ass like Dickens said. There are thousands of people all over the country living alone and some of them elderly. They're responsible people, not drop-outs or layabouts, and those seem to get hold of pistols anyway. The people I am thinking of wouldn't wave their guns about like cowboys. They'd use them to defend themselves and then only when they were really forced to."

"Another cup of tea?"

"Yes, please."

He used the moment while he made it to think again. This was an intelligent woman and her opinions were worth consideration. Finally he said deliberately: "It would make it difficult for the police, you know."

"I can't take that – they manage well enough in America. There it's the other way round, they tell me. Here you can't get a pistol legally without some very special reason. There anyone can have a gun provided he's sane and there's nothing against him."

"There's nothing in our constitution about a citizen's right to carry arms."

She nodded at once. "I've heard about that. But I don't think it really matters much." She waved an arm to comprehend Lexleigh. "How many people would get licences here? Twenty? Twenty-five? A hundred? The police would have a register, naturally. Are they so pushed that they couldn't check regularly? If some old boy has gone gently gaga they take his gun and that's the end of it."

"Administrative difficulties – "

"Pah!"

He reflected for the final time. "Do many of your friends feel like that?"

"I don't know a single one that doesn't."

He gave her her money and put on his hat. If he'd had

any doubts she had wholly resolved them. He was a respectable, pensioned government servant and he was going to do something entirely illegal.

He walked up the very slight rise to Wellworthy's house. In this Flanders-like country they called it Holland Hill. His hunt terrier went with him happily. She was very well trained and would wait in the porch and both of them welcomed the chance of exercise, she because she got bored in the house, he because hunt terriers, when they reached what he thought of as middle age, could get fat as pigs if you didn't walk them.

As he went Arthur Tribe reflected on Wellworthy. He had released him once from a merciless bullying and Wellworthy had been properly grateful. Would he be so still? Or grateful enough to do what Tribe wanted? If not Arthur Tribe had another weapon though it would go against the grain to use it.

When he had settled down in Lexleigh he hadn't known that Wellworthy lived there, and if he had it wouldn't have changed his decision. Lexleigh-on-Sea still thought of itself as rather grand – perhaps shabbily grand by now but still exclusive. In such a society you didn't bruit around that you had once been a sort of superior screw and it would simply have been grossly improper to disclose a piece of official knowledge, that one of its respected citizens had once been in your charge in prison. One or two other people might know but if they did they too had kept silent. For Wellworthy was now not only respectable but a man of solid influence locally; he was high in Rotary and a member of the local council. A builder seeking a necessary permission would be very unwise to invite his enmity. Under its air of faded grandeur Lexleigh was that sort of place at heart.

Harry Wellworthy had inherited the family business. A cousin had drowned off this treacherous coast and his father's will had left Harry next in line. The old man had been too stricken to change it or possibly he hadn't cared.

Wellworthy had been a household name and Harry the last male of the family.

Had been a household name but now was less so. For the business was importing bulbs and competition had eroded it sharply. Every house in the country which owned anything that could be called a garden still received Wellworthy's annual catalogue but it also saw others and some sold much cheaper. But Harry still lived in apparent state in a villa on the crest of Holland Hill. Arthur, as he sighted it, was extremely glad he didn't own it. Such a folly would eat up income remorselessly. It had been built in Lexleigh's highest heyday for a then famous actress, the mistress of a profligate duke. Today, Tribe thought, it was almost unsaleable. It wasn't a country house with land, nor big enough for an institution; its garden was small – too small for development. The only thing to do with it was to turn it into a block of flats and such conversions were two a penny in Lexleigh.

He rang the bell and an elderly maid in an apron let him in. In this declining resort there were still such survivals. He told the dog to sit and went in.

"Will you wait in the parlour, please."

The parlour! The word had been entirely appropriate.

As he waited Arthur Tribe weighed his chances. He wasn't on very close terms with Wellworthy but had played golf with him at the local club where Wellworthy was a solid Four, Arthur competent but nearer Ten; and occasionally they met outside it. But they had never been to each other's houses. For one thing Wellworthy had a formidable wife and for another Tribe could not afford to entertain back on the Wellworthy scale. But the two men were on easy terms. Tribe was within the social conventions in paying a call on Harry Wellworthy. Nevertheless he'd be surprised to see him.

Wellworthy came in and offered a drink. Tribe declined politely but firmly. He had some tricky talking to do and it wasn't yet noon. He had decided that, to start with at least, he'd be as straightforward as the matter allowed.

13

Wellworthy was saying amiably: "What can I do for you?"

"I've come to ask a favour."

"Why not? I owe you something more than a favour."

Rather better than so far so good, Tribe thought. He decided to cut a corner and did so. "I want you to get me a gun," he said.

Wellworthy's astonishment was immediate and genuine. "A gun?" he repeated blankly.

"A pistol."

"A pistol to protect yourself?"

"No."

"Then may I ask – "

"I'm afraid you may not."

"It all sounds a little dicey."

"It is."

Wellworthy went to the sideboard and mixed a drink, offering again to Arthur Tribe. This time he accepted gladly. His highest fence was now behind him, made unexpectedly easy by Wellworthy. There might be a bit of blackmail to come but though Tribe detested the smell of blackmail he must accept it in a cause he thought just. Wellworthy said: "Good health."

"The same to you."

"Which I shan't enjoy in prison again. If I start fiddling with illicit fire-arms – "

"Fiddling puts it much too high. Your bulbs are lorried down from Holland, then shipped across to the port of Sokenhoe. That's just round the corner from here and convenient. And guns are easily come by in Belgium."

Tribe watched Wellworthy frown in embarrassment. He had seen his record and had observed him in prison. He wasn't a hardened criminal; he was weak. Tribe had little sympathy with current theories of criminology but he had a natural, wholly personal, sympathy for a man whose stars had been set against him. Wellworthy's father had indulged expensive tastes; he had kept horses in a neighbouring hunt; he had taken a gun in a very grand syndicate.

14

The hunting had ended his life in an accident. He had only been forty-three and Harry twelve.

His widowed mother had promptly spoiled him outrageously. He had gone to the local public school, a tough one where he hadn't been happy, but in the holidays he could have what he wanted. Thereafter he'd drifted from job to job, losing most of them through some petty malfeasance. He had also gambled far beyond his means. Finally he had cheated a bookmaker and the whole weight of that unforgiving profession had been thrown against him, no holds barred. Harry Wellworthy had gone to prison.

Not an evil man, Tribe thought, but a natural criminal. He would always take the easy way and Arthur Tribe had high suspicions that this was what he was doing now. Which was his own second card if he had to use it. But it wasn't a certain winner, far from it: his suspicions, which he knew were shared, might be founded on nothing but local rumour. In which case the card would fall flat on the table. But if there were a grain of truth in what he and one or two others suspected, Wellworthy would get him that gun.

Meanwhile he watched Wellworthy's face intently. It had changed from astonishment first to resentment and then to a very evident fear. Finally he said bleakly: "No. I owe you a lot but you're asking too much. Guns are much too hot to handle."

"Unlike other things which I know you do handle." Tribe hated himself as he said it but he spoke.

Wellworthy rose from his chair for another drink, turning his back on Tribe as he went for it. He did so as much to hide his face as for another drink which he did not need. He didn't offer a second to Arthur Tribe. He took a pull at his own and then put it down; he returned to his chair and said almost casually: "How much do you know, Arthur Tribe?"

. . . He may be a small-time crook but he's not a coward.

"How much do I know? Enough to put you back in prison."

"A largish claim. Tell me what you've got on me."

He's pretty cool, Tribe thought. I rather like him and I hate myself.

"To tell you that would be poor technique. Do you mind if I smoke?"

"If you must. My wife hates it. Whatever you do don't drop ash on the carpet."

"Then may I have an ashtray, please?"

Wellworthy brought one and Tribe went on. "Then let's consider the background locally. This coast was made by God for smuggling – half a dozen little decaying ports and saltings where you can land in a dinghy provided you don't get caught by the tide. It's impossible to police all of it and Customs takes a sensible attitude. Provided the big stuff doesn't come in here – heroin, for instance, or illegal immigrants – "

"Guns would be big stuff."

"Not a single gun wouldn't."

"You have a semantic point. Go on."

"So Customs does what it must which is play it cool. I would guess that they realise what's going on but to stamp it out would need an army and they're kept on a very tight rein for money. The occasional pounce, of course, but little more. And maybe there's another factor."

"What?"

"There's a Customs training school just up the coast. Stamp out smuggling entirely – petty smuggling – and where do you train your men to their job?"

"You could send them to Heathrow or Liverpool."

"Throw them in at the deep end? Poor training."

"You seem to have thought it out."

"Maybe."

"And something else. You're a shameless blackmailer."

"Running a prison you do get crafty."

"Evidently," Harry Wellworthy said. "So what's the proposition, please. I'd like to have it clear and settled."

"You get me that gun and that's the end of it."

"Of what?"

"Of what I know."

"I have your word?"

"For what it's worth to you."

"I happen to think it's worth a lot."

"I thank you for that."

"Then just one gun?"

"One gun is plenty, thank you kindly."

Miss Janet Clegg had come down from the North and had kept most of her Lancashire candour and bite. She was an efficient nurse, as crisp as a biscuit, and she still thought most Southerners soft as putty. She had a strong sense of independence, too, which had prevented her rising to where she might have. There had been men in her life but no one serious. She had trained in London, then moved to East Anglia for she had never felt quite at home in the capital. She had greatly preferred her East Anglian town where the people were almost as forthright as herself.

Now she was in contented retirement. She had a pension and a modest inheritance and she lived in comfort if not in style in a terraced house which still had some character. She was liked and respected and there she intended to die.

And one morning she very nearly did. Prematurely. It was a mile from her house to where she shopped and Janet Clegg enjoyed the walk. Or had until she'd been brutally mugged and left in the gutter with face and ribs broken. For once there had been a reliable witness and the police had been able to bring men to trial. They had been sentenced with an offensive leniency since they'd belonged to an overprivileged class, students from a new Commonwealth country. She'd been severely hurt but had stubbornly healed. Now she was back at home at last, the threads of her humdrum life in her hands again. The incident had shaken her badly but it hadn't destroyed her Northern guts.

She rose as she heard the front door bell ring. That will be the milkman, she thought. At other houses he simply left bottles but she had guessed that he'd been quietly asked to keep a daily eye on her welfare.

But it wasn't the milk: it was the post. She didn't get very much of that and what she did came rattling through the box onto the floor. But today the postman had rung and was waiting. "Parcel for you today," he said. He held it out.

Janet Clegg received few parcels and she looked at it with a certain doubt. She read her papers and had heard of, well, happenings. "I suppose it isn't a bomb," she said.

The postman laughed. "Were you expecting one?"

Janet didn't answer this but she had the caution of her Lancashire blood and knowledge which the postman, not a local, didn't share. Two men had mugged her and gone to prison. Not for nearly long enough but to prison they had duly gone. They wouldn't be out yet but if they had friends . . .

Janet Clegg took two newspapers daily, one for the news and one for the titbits. She had heard of criminal gangs and of revenge.

The postman decided he'd waited long enough; he also decided he'd humour this madwoman. He shook the parcel vigorously. Nothing happened. The postman seemed to think he'd proved something. "This isn't a bomb," he said politely. He held the parcel out again. Janet hesitated but she finally took it.

"Good morning, mum."

"Good morning, postie."

She took the parcel inside to the kitchen. The postmark was blurred and she couldn't be sure of it. It looked like somewhere in north London's wilderness. But that meant nothing. She took off the brown paper gingerly. Under it was a stout cardboard box. She hesitated again but opened that too. Inside was a brand new revolver and six rounds.

She was a woman who made her decisions quickly. A little late, she thought, but I'll keep it. Her house still kept a certain character but the area was going down fast. She'd been assaulted once and you never knew, so she didn't waste time in speculation. Someone unknown had sent her a weapon, someone who must be sympathetic.

Janet Clegg was going to keep it.

18

Under the gun were carefully typed instructions. The writer presented respectful compliments and would be grateful if she would read this attentively. The revolver was Belgian and in his opinion distinctly shoddy. He would have preferred an automatic which at least would have had a proper safety catch. With this thing you simply loaded the chambers but to fire it you had to cock the hammer. That you never did till you wanted to fire. And if madam had been watching Westerns you never, but never, behaved like the sheriff. Cock the hammer and hold the pistol with both hands. Like the police. Maybe she'd seen that on the box too. Take a deep breath and hold it. Squeeze the trigger firmly. Don't snatch.

And the best of British luck to you.

So when the thief came in Janet Clegg was ready. He wasn't a professional and had made more noise than a good thief would have. In any case Janet Clegg slept lightly. She had the revolver under her pillow and cocked it. Then she turned on the bedside light and sat up.

Under the bedroom door the thief had seen a light. He was surprised but he came on with a shrug. He knew he was robbing a woman who lived alone.

He opened the door and faced a gun.

He stopped to think it over, but confidently. There was a woman sitting up in bed and that woman was holding a fire-arm properly. But elderly women very seldom kept fire-arms. Probably it was only a dummy and if it were not the odds were still with him. She wouldn't have the nerve to pull and if she did she was likely to miss him.

In which case he'd make her pay dearly for the act. The thief came on.

Janet had remembered her meticulous instructions. She had already cocked and now drew a deep breath. She held it and squeezed the trigger gently. She had never fired a fire-arm before but her shot drilled the thief through the heart like a marksman's. He fell on his face by the single bed.

Janet Clegg got out of it. She didn't need to examine him to know that he was dead. She'd been a nurse.

19

She sat down on the bed to think it over. She was shrewd as well as fiercely decisive; she knew no law but she read two newspapers and she knew that you couldn't just shoot men down as though they were game. That they had broken in and might rob and maim you wasn't enough. She would have liked to search the body for arms but decided against it. Some clever policeman might spot the search and if she found nothing she'd be no further forward.

Janet put on her dressing-gown, walking steadily to her spotless kitchen. There she coolly made a pot of tea, then went towards her knife-box reflectively. She had decided on her carving knife, a formidable affair with a serrated edge. She had often wondered that in the nanny State such things were freely available everywhere. Some busybody should have passed some law for them.

She put on her kitchen gloves and took it out, then she went back to her bedroom thoughtfully. The thief was still on his face, very dead.

She put the knife in his right hand and closed it. She put her gloves back in the drawer where they belonged. Then she rang the police and asked for help.

While they were coming she dressed herself carefully. One didn't receive strange men in a dressing-gown.

2

The Security Executive had been quietly reorganised since the days when it had been the obedient instrument of the Major, now Colonel, whom Arthur Tribe had remembered. An intelligent Prime Minister had shaped it as a Board of Directors. He himself would take the chair in crises, an arrangement which saved him valuable time since a crisis would have to come up to him anyway and he much preferred to hear men talking than read papers in the gobbledegook which in Whitehall had displaced the English language. The Colonel still came in twice a week advising when he was asked to – not otherwise – but the Executive was now run like a business, the directors controlling its operations.

These hadn't changed much except in emphasis and could still be defined as counter-subversion, subversion in its turn more widely as anything which endangered the State. What that would mean in daily practice would vary with a government's policy but since this could swing from wet Right to hard Left the field of possible intervention grew larger as each swing grew wider. The ability to intervene depended on knowledge of how to do so and there were people who would have been much surprised if they had known that the Executive held an up-to-date and growing file on them. Every man had if not his price at least his own peculiar weakness so that action, when it had to be taken, needn't be taken in fumbling blindness. Thereafter the dust would be swept under the carpet. The Executive was manned by efficient professionals.

One of these was William Wilberforce Smith who had worked his way onto the Board by plain merit. He had been recruited by the Colonel himself and at the time the appointment had been called controversial. Willy could well have had clashing loyalties but the Colonel was a shrewd judge of men and if they carried what seemed a disadvantage was prepared to look under their skins at the man below. In Willy he had chosen well. As an operator he had been bold and effective and later, as a desk man, intelligent. So now he was on the Board itself waiting for a man called Mark Hassall.

Who wasn't, Willy reflected quietly, so different from himself in essentials. He too had risen fast and by merit and was now a Superintendent of Police, young for the rank but still marked for promotion. Willy had met him before and had been impressed.

He had seen a man whom he couldn't quite place. He spoke well, without a hint of the Greater London whine, but rather with a faint West Country burr. He was wearing plain clothes which he wore with confidence and a cricket club tie which Willy recognised. He had then been a sharp-looking Chief Inspector and his family, Willy Smith decided, might perhaps have been a little surprised that he'd chosen the police instead of the army. Light Infantry at an intelligent guess – the West Country was one of its major recruiting grounds. That was no doubt speculation but one thing was clear beyond a question: this was the New Policeman in person. If politics tilted really Left he'd die in a concentration camp or, if he were exceptionally lucky, be put against a wall and shot; but if they moved Right he might go anywhere, perhaps as the head of a national police force under a Minister prepared to use it.

Now he was facing Willy Smith. Willy had never worked with him formally but both men played club cricket regularly and held each other in proper respect.

Willy had been mildly surprised when Hassall had rung for an urgent interview. Hassall's current job was anomalous, something between the Regular Drug Squad and what was formally called the Special Branch but in the

22

Force itself was often known otherwise. Drugs were not the Executive's business unless some Minister were hooked on heroin but the boundaries of the Special Branch could often overlap the Executive's. So Willy said: "Why, Mark! What brings you here? I thought you were in Drugs. Or officially."

"I am. But also liaising with H.M. Customs. You don't suppose Customs work quite alone?"

"And the Coastguards?"

Hassall laughed. "One thing Coastguards don't do is guard the coasts. They haven't done that for over a century."

"You're being a little Delphic."

"I'm sorry. So Customs watch things other than drugs. Guns, for instance. Guns would be very much your business."

"In quantity they certainly would. Is that happening? Really large-scale gun-running?"

"No. Or not yet."

"Then you're going too fast."

Mark Hassall produced a folded newspaper, handing it across to Willy. The headline was a screamer, and read: OAP SLAYS INTRUDER.

"That's a local, of course, where it's red-hot news. But it made the national Press less flamboyantly."

"I saw it," Willy said. "What went on?"

"It was exactly what it seemed for once. This old girl had a gun and she aimed it straight."

"What will happen to her?"

Mark Hassall shrugged. "Nothing too dreadful, I'd hope – there'll be sympathy." He said what Arthur Tribe had thought. "Plenty of people think the present law foolish, or rather that it's too strictly administered; they'd like to see elderlies allowed to keep guns especially when they're living alone and provided that they're respectable people. So an elderly with an unauthorised pistol will hardly incur the law's full fury. And the man did have an ugly knife. In America what they call a Grand Jury would be likely to throw out all charges but one, that of possessing an unlicensed weapon. Here she'll have to face the music but I doubt if the Crown will press it hard and on any charge connected with killing she'll probably get a suspended sentence, very possibly get no conviction at all if her lawyer really pulls the stops out and the jury is sympathetic too. And a lot depends on the Judge – how he handles them. So I'm pretty sure she won't go to prison though she'll certainly face a fine for having the gun. A swingeing fine, I imagine." He laughed. "Which her friends will pass the hat round to pay. She was very well liked and respected locally."

"So it's open and shut?"

"Except for a trifle. The dead man was holding the knife in his right hand. He happened to be left-handed at all times."

"Unfortunate," Willy said.

"Very damaging to Janet Clegg."

"Will that be brought into Court?"

"No comment. But I told you she was well liked and respected."

"I apologise. I shouldn't have asked."

"It was well below your normal form. Apology accepted, though."

"Then what about the gun itself?"

"Very curious indeed, a bit sinister. You and I know that illegal guns go washing around like Arab money. There's a pub in Soho where you can buy one for two hundred. And a very poor bargain you'll get for your money. To begin with what you'll buy will be hot – used in some other crime already. It will also be very poorly maintained. I know of a case of a man who bought one. The first time he fired it he lost his hand."

"Justice of a sort."

"Rough justice. But Janet Clegg's gun was brand new and Belgian. She says she got it by post and anonymously."

"Have the police been working on that?"

"Of course. But they've come to a complete dead end. Clegg naturally burnt the wrapping – not that that would have helped the police much – but she kept the instructions which came with the pistol. They'd been typed with the sort of cheap machine which you can buy in any high street shop and the paper was equally common and useless. So Janet Clegg gets a gun from she doesn't know where. That's her story and she sticks to it firmly."

"The police believe her?"

"I think they must. They ask themselves a single question: how else could she get a brand new gun if some sympathiser hadn't sent it her?"

Willy Smith had been watching Hassall as he talked. He talked smoothly and well but he wasn't a chatterbox; he hadn't paid this call just to gossip. Willy gave him more time but he didn't go on. Finally Willy had to prompt him.

"I don't suppose you called on us to discuss a woman shooting a burglar."

"Perfectly correct and perceptive. I've called for two reasons and I'll take them in order. The gun was Belgian – in passing, shoddy – and there's still a good deal of coastal traffic between that string of little east Essex ports and the half dozen on the Belgian coast. Tramp steamers and even motorised barges."

"So the gun came in from Belgium. What of it?"

"Because if it did it was *smuggled* in. That's the second reason I've come to see you. Those broken-down Essex havens are a smuggler's paradise. They always have been – there's a local tradition. You know the sort of thing I mean – brandy, tobacco, scent, the luxuries. I talked about tradition and it has survived. *Watch the wall, my darling, As the gentlemen go by.*"

He had smiled as he quoted and now went on. "Customs with whom I work suspect it but they haven't the man-power to stamp it out. They have bigger things to think of, such as drugs."

"Then drugs don't come in through these Essex harbours?"

"So far I gather they haven't – no."

"But you suspect a gun has. One gun . . ."

"Where one gun comes in a flood could follow. That's why I've come to the Security Executive. Janet Clegg's gun is no business of yours but flood an inner city with fire-arms and a government could fall tomorrow." Hassall stopped for breath. "I've earned a drink."

"Only the boss is supposed to keep it. There is booze in his desk but I don't dare raid it."

"Then we'll have to go to a pub."

"Lead on."

Hassall led Willy out with confidence taking a cab to a pub called The Boot. It was old-fashioned, untarted, comfortable and too hot. There were booths along the southern wall where a couple could talk without interruption. Willy led Mark Hassall to the bar.

"What will you have?"

"A pint of bitter beer, if I may."

Willy tried not to laugh but gave it up. "It does sound a little grand like that. I thought the police slang for a pint was a jar."

"You've been goggling the box too much. When I want a pint of bitter beer I ask for a pint of bitter beer. And I see you're having gin and tonic. Good luck to you, you've earned it by listening. In fact I'd much prefer one too but I'm known in this pub and I have to be careful. If I were seen to be drinking gin before lunch it would be noticed and on the odds reported."

"Reported that you were a soak?"

"Not at all. It isn't the gin it's the money to pay for it. I'd be suspect of being as bent as a corkscrew. There's a campaign, you know, about police corruption. It's orchestrated and it's also subsidised. I imagine you know the sort who run it."

"They try to smear the Executive too."

"Little paragraphs, Parliamentary Questions, plain lies.

26

Police corruption, police abuse of powers. Picking up some layabout hophead. Pulling in some pusher of heroin if he happens to be Greek or Asian. I see you know the people I mean."

"Let's not mention them."

"Gladly."

Mark Hassall lit a cigarette, offering one to Willy who declined. He would have preferred a couple of drags on a reefer, a drug which he used with the strictest discipline. His race had used marijuana for centuries, quite as long as Mark Hassall's had fancied alcohol. Over-indulgence in that was degrading and pot could wreck a life as effectively. But Hassall could use drink intelligently and Willy was properly cautious with smoking. What was the difference between civilised men?

The difference was that Mark was a policeman and this was no place to embarrass him publicly.

Willy put back his silver case. Hassall noticed it and said with mild envy: "That's a beautiful thing."

"Amanda gave it me." He didn't say when or why: that was private. In fact it had been when she'd borne their second child. Usually it was the other way round, the proud father giving his wife a present. This Willy Smith had done and generously for his father had left him a handsome competence derived from a shrewd knowledge of property. But his wife had got in first with the silver case. She had badly wanted a second son and Willy had obliged her successfully.

He had used the time while Hassall smoked to think, for Hassall had spoken of floods of arms which would turn already restive slums into no-go fortresses tighter than Ulster's. Willy was a little sceptical. That had been tried before and beaten, and tried by men much more powerful than smugglers. It might be tried again and perhaps succeed but it wouldn't succeed for long – it couldn't. In Ulster there were special circumstances: religion and American sympathy inhibited the obvious action. Here an armed enclave would not be tolerated. Two companies

27

of reliable infantry would go through untrained men like butter . . .

And two companies of reliable infantry would in doing so bring down any government in a day. Willy said softly, feeling his way: "You were talking about large-scale smuggling of arms. You mentioned the inner cities – "

"Yes. And I wasn't as clear as perhaps I should have been. We both of us know that's been tried before and we both of us know it was blocked – you blocked it. It was a political ploy and the Executive took it on. I was thinking of something more on my side and I was thinking of something bigger than small arms."

"Something bigger than small arms? In whose hands?"

"In a common criminal's hands," Hassall said.

"You're serious?"

"I'm afraid I am. Organised crime today is sophisticated. It's a silly word, really – it just means complicated – but it also means we must follow developments and there are very firm limits on what we can do."

"Illustrate," Willy said.

"I will. Take an average raid on some major target, say an armoured van which is carrying bullion. Current form is to wait till a guard gets out, then grab him and soak the poor brute in petrol. You wave matches or a lighter at him and sooner or later he gives you the keys. All this takes time and may well go wrong. And if the load is official and sufficiently valuable the van will have a proper escort."

"It's been done, though."

"With very careful planning. And luck. A good deal of luck. What I'm afraid of is the elimination of the luck. Time is of the essence in any raid. Cut that down and you cut down the chances against you."

"How?"

"Blow the van with an AP rocket. Loot it. A single escape car. No hanging about."

Willy thought it over, said: "I can see that would be awkward. Too easy."

"You've acquired a taste for understatement."

"But who's going to do this thing?"

"Some big boy. If I talked about master criminals you'd rightly laugh. But rich ones exist since crime does pay. They're not the men who commit the crimes but the men who stand behind and finance them. Rather like Krupps and Hitler."

"Prettily put."

"Have you ever heard of a man called Marcos?"

Willy shook his head. "I have not."

"He has one of those polysyllabic Greek names which nobody can get their tongues round but he's happy enough to be called just Marcos. He's a Cypriot Greek – in prison once but never again. He saw where the real money lay and went for it. Now he's behind the big ones – most of them."

Willy had been taught to go slowly. "I've no more than the normal knowledge of how big crime works but take your hypothetical case, the load of gold. Let's say it's worth a couple of million. But the men who lift it don't get two million. There are the crooked jewellers to melt it down and when it has finally lost its markings it has still to be turned into usable cash. I know that it isn't all that easy to turn unidentified gold into twenty-pound notes. You need a dealer in bullion – "

"Precisely my point. The Marcoses take care of all that and keep at least forty per cent for doing it."

"All right. You know more than I do. Go on. What connection has this Marcos of yours with petty smuggling through an east coast harbour?"

Hassall said coolly: "Almost none. But enough to make a policeman curious. Curious enough to come round to you."

"I'm listening," Willy said.

"Then here it is. There are only two established facts: that somewhere on that coast there's some smuggling and that one of the men in a position to do so and who lives in a place called Lexleigh-on-Sea has criminal form.

He's called Harry Wellworthy and he's been in prison. In a way he was rather unlucky to go there and he's been blameless as far as we know since he came out. He inherited the family business which is importing bulbs from Holland through Belgium and is now something of a local notable. The bulbs come in in hundredweight sacks. You can get other things than bulbs in a hundredweight sack."

"Why should this Wellworthy want to do so?"

"Because his business is extremely rocky. It had nearly a monopoly once, now it has a hard time keeping alive."

"So this Wellworthy makes a bit on the side. Soft contraband, I believe they call it."

"It could turn hard."

"But has it?"

"I don't know."

Willy knew Hassall well, could speak freely. "It's a web of conjecture. I think that's the accepted phrase."

"It's the accepted phrase with third-class barristers but it's all a poor policeman has to go on. Except in this particular case." He sat up suddenly. *"Wellworthy was in prison with Marcos."*

Willy's manner changed sharply from doubt to interest but he thought carefully before he spoke. "If I've got this right it goes something like this. You're not interested in small-time smuggling, not even the occasional gun. Customs can deal with that if they have to. What you're interested in is the growth potential – AP rockets and other toys. You name them."

"It's your turn to have put it prettily."

"All right. So Marcos gets together with Wellworthy and starts to run in dangerous playthings. That's a difference of degree but not of kind. It still wouldn't be any part of my business."

"In that I think you're greatly mistaken. A rocket through some Minister's car . . . Or someone grander than an unpopular Minister. That would be political and you're paid to keep an eye on politics. At the least you'd be asked is why you gave no warning."

"You're trying to frighten me, " Willy said. "You have. Give me a minute to think."

"As long as you like."

Willy took a full five minutes for he had more to consider than Hassall knew. Hassall had his information and Willy had his – from different sources. Hassall knew all about men like Marcos and Willy had known nothing at all, but Marcos, as Hassall had said, was a criminal and Willy wasn't paid to fight common crime; he was fed to defeat subversion in all of its nowadays protean forms and the most consistent of these, the most immediately dangerous, was naked and increasing terrorism.

And in this shadowy but terrifying world something was stirring, the really big one. Willy didn't know what but the mountain was labouring and it wouldn't be a mouse at the birth . . . "A rocket through some Minister's car . . . Or someone grander than an unpopular Minister . . ."

Willy didn't attempt to define his fear but asked a single straight question. "If your Marcos brought in more than side arms would he deal with men who weren't ordinary criminals?"

"He would if there were money in it – yes."

"Then tell me what we can do to help you."

Hassall let out his breath in a silent sigh; he had got what he had come for and said: "I'd like a second opinion, please."

"On what goes on in those Essex saltings? I'll send a good man to Lexleigh at once."

"I'd rather have your opinion than his."

Willy stared at him in real astonishment. "Mark, you must be out of your mind. In Lexleigh I'd stand out like a canker."

"That's very superficial thinking. You are, since you force me to mention it, black, but in every other imaginable way you'd fit Lexleigh like the proverbial glove."

"You're talking utter balls."

31

"I am not. You speak English rather better than I do. Maybe they taught you that at Harrow." Hassall grinned. "I don't know – I wasn't there. And you have the manner of an English gentleman. Whatever that may mean today."

Willy was pleased but he wasn't flattered. He thought of himself when he did so at all, not so much as an English gentleman but as an Englishman of the professional class whose face happened to be handsomely black. That was a fact but by now inconsiderable. He knew men who were ashamed of their colour and others who waved it about like a flag. Willy thought both of them equally tiresome.

Hassall was repeating firmly: "You'd be perfectly at home in Lexleigh. It has something of the grand manner still."

"Why do I go there?"

"You go on holiday. I know you're due for a fortnight's leave."

"You've been spying on me," Willy said.

"If you call that spying. I call it homework."

"We were thinking of somewhere a good deal warmer than Lexleigh."

"You'd be bored to death on a beach."

Willy nodded a reluctant agreement. He loved the sun but idleness irked him and they would have to fly a long way for real sun. "What about Amanda, though? Amanda will be disappointed."

"But she'll agree in the end if she sees you're set on it."

"How do you know?"

"I've met Amanda."

Willy was tempted and let Hassall see it. It was true that he was due for a break; things were quiet at the office; he could go when he pleased. "And the snags?" he enquired. "There are always snags."

"In this case I see no snags whatever. Take a room at the Clarence. Better a modest suite. In February you'll get one easily. Swan about a bit, if you know what I mean. They'll take you for some African diplomat provided you hide that you're much too intelligent."

32

"Will Amanda like the Clarence?"

"I think so. It's solidly comfortable in the high British manner. No ice in the water unless you ask for it."

"I'll talk to her, then."

"You do just that."

3

Willy had said he would talk to his wife but he hadn't been sure she'd agree about Lexleigh. She had an emotional attachment to Brighton and with some reason. Both her children had started life there, the first before they'd been formally married when in effect she had carried him off and seduced him and the second three years later with an equal gusto but greater propriety. They were now lusty boys at a preparatory school which would take them for a fortnight as boarders whichever resort their parents fancied. Willy was old-fashioned and scrupulous and a holiday couldn't be charged to expenses simply because Mark Hassall had urged it; but though he was very British by now and would have been embarrassed by any suggestion of privilege he earned the salary of an Assistant Secretary as a member of the Executive's Board and the competence which his father had left him was helpful in such expensive extras as sending two boys to a private prep school. Later, of course, they'd go on to Harrow where at least they'd learn to play cricket respectably. There wasn't any reason whatever why Amanda and Willy shouldn't lodge at the Clarence.

Nevertheless William Wilberforce Smith had expected some opposition from his wife. She was an excellent housewife which meant a creature of habit . . . They had always gone to the south coast so why not now? But also she could read Willy perfectly and she had sensed the malaise of a certain restlessness. He had been recruited as an operator and as an operator he had worked his way up from mere legwork to quite responsible missions. By now he was on the Board, well thought of, and it wasn't quite impossible that with luck he would one day become its head. Amanda was very properly proud of him but she was

34

also his wife and obliged to live with him. When restless he could often be irritable and she knew that he missed the rough and tumble of an operator's varied life. He too was a man of disciplined habit and he had suddenly changed from Brighton to Lexleigh. Amanda had privately smiled but said nothing. Her guess was that this change had a reason. To Londoners Lexleigh-on-Sea was 'abroad' but if the holiday had some other reason than merely an itch for somewhere new Amanda would very happily welcome it. A change from office work would do Willy good.

Amanda Smith was a very nice woman.

They had been received at the Clarence precisely as Willy Smith would have wished – courteously but without curiosity. It was a solid old place still in family hands, perhaps a little tatty but comfortable. Service was with a smile, given willingly. They had taken a bedroom with a very small sitting room and both looked across a stretch of lawn to the ever-restless sea below them. The other residents, Willy saw, were civilised; they gave you good morning and didn't stare. To this opinion he would have made one exception, a couple of Arabs he considered showed off. Which in Willy's ethos was the unforgivable sin. They wore their robes at all times and swished them. They were down in the hotel register as *Merchants* but Willy rather more than suspected that they hadn't come to Lexleigh-on-Sea to trade.

And one day he'd had a very slight brush with them. They had been sweeping down the hall together and Willy had been going the other way. They had clearly expected that Willy would step aside. Why not? In Arabic there was a very rude word for Willy Smith. He had walked straight on and they had visibly hesitated. Finally they had parted and let him through.

Willy went up to his room and a rare brandy. It had been a very small triumph and wholly contemptible. By now he was entirely assimilated; he was innocent of racial prejudice and he mistrusted overworked words like sub-conscious. But deep in that misty, over-fashionable organ lay instinctive distrust and dislike of Arabs. These men had sold his forbears to slavery: now they were fortuitously rich. Their money swirled round the West like their robes and, unlike those showy things, did active harm.

Willy finished his drink and recovered his temper, writing the incident off for ever. But he had read a good deal of modern history and it reinforced his firm opinion that the destruction of the Ottoman empire had been the greatest mistake of a century full of them.

Next morning he did his first reconnaissance, walking round Lexleigh, getting the feel of it. The station was served by a single line, one side of it closed, the other dilapidated. A single train an hour ran each way. It was enough. Beyond the station was what was called the New Town. This was where the multiple stores were and streets of bungalows of no great character. It might have been a development any-where. But south of the railway lay Lexleigh proper, hardly grand any more but still consciously decorous. There were one or two enormous houses which with land would have rated as country estates, but the average was a well-built villa, a holiday home or a place for retirement, on the straight avenues which ran down to the sea. Now many were split into two or more flats but they had once been owned by Generals and Admirals, retired Governors of colonial provinces, the upper crust of what had then been an empire.

Willy looked at them with a real nostalgia. Edwardian was now a dirty word, or was with the sort of people he disliked. It was their synonym for vulgar but it was wrong. Granted those preposterous house parties where the men spent their time in slaughtering birds; where the women spent theirs in repetitive gossip or envying each other's jewellery; where the servants sat down in their masters' precedence – granted all this it was by no means the whole of it. There was security, the Pax Britannica. Nobody murdered political dissidents, aircraft weren't highjacked for senseless reasons. No doubt the poor were poorer and dirtier, the rich contemptuous of social conscience, but given that you weren't on the breadline it was arguable that you were happier then than fighting what was called the class war. Willy realised that this was unfashionable thinking but he could smell the cigars and the brandies and soda and he rather liked the aroma of both.

And Lexleigh's peculiar flavour apart it was a well laid out and agreeable seaside town. There was no tarmacked promenade – that *would* have been vulgar – but a row of houses, its centre the Clarence. Between them and the sea was an ordinary road and a long sward of grass kept surprisingly green in the bitter east winds. The grass in turn dropped suddenly to the sea, twenty feet perhaps, and almost vertically. Below was a row of bathing chalets, substantial affairs since they had to be so, but once in a generation at least a storm would smash the whole file to matchwood. You weren't supposed to sleep in them but the rule was not enforced too severely provided the sleepers were quiet and clean. As most visitors to Lexleigh were. A few miles down the coast was the monstrous Gleaville but its patrons were entirely different. They would have thought these chalets offensively posh and would have vandalised the lot at sight. One or two of them even had telephones.

Willy, when he had seen them first, had started to hum. His father had had a fine baritone voice and had been fond of the music hall tunes of his time.

Oh, I do like to be beside the seaside (Bom)
Oh, I do like to be beside the sea (Bom, bom)
Oh, I do like to stroll along the prom, prom, prom
Where the brass band plays
Tiddily om, pom, pom
Oh, I do like to be beside the seaside (Bom)
Oh, I do like to be beside the sea-ee-ee
There are lots of girls beside
I would like to be astride
Beside the seaside (Bom)
Beside the sea.

Over luncheon Willy Smith told Amanda: "I hope you weren't bored this morning."

"Not at all. I went shopping."

Her husband hid an instinctive smile since to have shown it would have been crudely macho. But shopping, he was thinking – shopping! What on earth could the woman want in the shops? The boys were safely away at school, the maids did their room, the hotel was feeding them. The word was almost ritualistic. She'd have been looking in the windows and chatting. "Buy anything?" he inquired.

"These shoes." She put out an ankle. It had a fine baroque curve.

"I noticed them," Willy said.

"You're a liar."

They both of them laughed but she collected her winnings. "Just to pay you out for being blind they cost me a terrible lot of money."

"Just so long as you're the good girl you have been. I'm going to leave you tomorrow morning too."

"I didn't suppose you came to Lexleigh because you'd been reading the ads. There aren't any."

"What was that?"

"Don't be dim. I've been married to you ten years. You're on a job."

This time he let her see his smile. "You're a very shrewd number."

"I've a certain experience. So what's it all about?"

He could tell her since she never gossiped. "Smuggling," he said.

"That's no business of yours."

"It could be if they smuggled the wrong things."

"Through Lexleigh?"

"Not through Lexleigh. But this coast is riddled with inlets and estuaries and most of them have little harbours. Some of them have silted up, some have been turned into yacht marinas, but a few still have some vestige of trade. Within sixty miles of Lexleigh, either side, I reckon there are half a dozen."

"Where will you start?"

"At the nearest, of course. It's called Sokenhoe and still sometimes does business."

"Then meet me for lunch at a place called Barbara's. I found it this morning and liked the look of it." She added on a faint note of mockery: "When I was doing the shopping, you know."

Willy was good at reading maps and could get from them a very fair picture of what he would see when he reached the ground. Between Lexleigh and Sokenhoe lay a saddle of rising land. It was barely more than a hump in the ground but in this flat Netherlands country was called the Mount. Beyond it where the contours flattened again was a creek and whatever was left of Sokenhoe. Willy had decided what to do: he'd go to Sokenhoe itself tomorrow but it was better to get the wider picture first. He would walk to the top of the hump and use glasses. There was a bridleway shown on his map and he'd take it. It also showed a footbridge across the creek.

The hump was under cultivation and Willy, though a townsman, looked at the crop. Rape, he was inclined to think, but not the type they grew for seed oil. Later they'd put it down to silage or maybe just plough it in for the humus. Afterwards would come spring barley. Willy walked on.

At the top of the rise he took out his glasses, looking around him, quietly absorbing. To his left was the sea, contained by a high and very Dutch-looking dyke, and below the dyke a sort of polder. It was now a golf course and looked a boring one. At its centre was a squat white building which Willy knew from the map was the local pumping station. Yes, the Dutch had been here, the great masters of water. There was a Holland Road or a Holland Avenue in every township along this vulnerable coast. Willy swung his glasses right on a village which he wasn't surprised was called Breda. It had a manor though no sign of life around it and a fine perpendicular church which would have been more at home in a West Country village than in this sea-threatened soke of marsh and saltings. Willy finally centred his glasses on Sokenhoe.

It was much as he had expected but more so, a smallish port which had once been prosperous but was now in all too evident decline. There was a line of visibly crumbling warehouses and a single jetty still left standing. At the jetty was a motorised barge. That was all. Sprinkle the landscape with broken arches, with picturesque peasants in attitudes more so and a French romantic painter would have done it in his sleep. Behind the ruins stood the Martello tower.

Willy had noticed the shooting-hides as he climbed. They were holes in the ground half-concealed by canvas screens or brushwood, evidently for sportsmen after fowl. There was one where he stood on the bridleway and Willy decided he'd take a look. He had begun to move when a man stepped out of it. He had a shotgun which he pointed at Willy. "Stop," he said. "Don't talk. Stand still."

Willy Smith obeyed him promptly.

For a moment they stood in silence, both wary. The man wore the local uniform, high rubber boots and a soft cloth cap. Finally he said: "Who are you?"

"My name is William Smith."

"And what are you doing here?"

"I was watching the birds."

It was the truth but not all of it. On the salting below he'd seen pochard and mallard and one of Willy's interests was birds. In the garden of their house in Wimbledon he kept a birdbath and a table to feed from. The one was always clean, the other supplied. He held out his glasses to prove his point.

The man seemed a little mollified, said: "You're trespassing too." The words were rough but the accent was not.

"I didn't know that. The map shows a bridleway."

"Look at your bloody map again. There's a side-note which says that a right of way shown isn't proof that a right of way still exists."

"This one is closed?"

"Not yet but we're trying to. So anyone successfully using it would be evidence against us in Court. Let's say this right of way's in desuetude."

. . . "Desuetude" indeed! Very odd. This man wasn't dressed to say "desuetude."

Both men were watching the other intently. The situation was static and could end in one of two ways. One would be disagreeable for Willy. To break the deadlock he said politely: "So you want to close this bridlepath down. To do so you carry a loaded shotgun." It was a dangerous thing to say but he had to move. There was something about this man which wasn't right. Willy Smith didn't think he'd shoot to kill but he might pepper your legs with Number Eight.

To his surprise the man with the shotgun laughed loudly. "The gun is a deterrent, yes, but has another use besides frightening trespassers. You see these hides all round us?"

"Yes." Willy noticed that the gun hadn't wavered.

"They're for me to protect this rape from the birds. I spend boring hours cooped up inside one of them."

"Those duck?" Willy asked.

"No, not those duck. But a gaggle of geese would strip these fields in two hours." He looked at Willy hard again, then apparently he made up his mind. "We've been standing here gossiping more than long enough." The manner changed back to uncouthness suddenly. "Get the hell out of here and do it fast."

"I'll go down the way I came."

"You will not. I told you that path was closed. You should listen." He waved an arm at the sea. "Down there." To point he had lowered the gun to the trail and for a moment Willy considered jumping him. But there wasn't any point in that now. "Work your way down the slope till you come to the golf course. Walk across that and you'll reach the dyke. There's a path along the top which will take you back to Lexleigh the long way round."

"And that one's still open?"

41

"Oh, go to hell. And try not to trample this rape as you go there. You may not think it's worth a lot but if those geese got at it I'd lose my job."

"Good morning, then."

"Hold your tongue and get moving."

Willy picked his way in the furrows carefully till cultivation began to merge into golf course. A couple of women golfers stared at him but nobody offered a challenge or hindrance. When he came to the dyke he climbed up by the flight of steps. The dyke was a substantial affair – it would have to be, Willy thought, with that sea. It was twenty to thirty feet high and tapered. Along the top was the established right of way.

It was deserted as Willy Smith climbed up to it except for a single man with a dog. He had stopped to watch Willy come up the concrete steps; they were steep and Willy had stumbled; he held out his hand. "Good morning," he said politely.

"Thank you."

Willy looked at the dog as it sat obediently. "Genuine, copper-bottomed hunt terrier. Not one of those rather stupid Jack Russells."

The man looked pleased. "You know the difference? Most people do not. What dog do you keep yourself?"

"I don't. I'd like to but I live in London."

"Considerate," the man said. "And fair. Fair to the wretched dog, I mean." He looked at Willy and smiled. "My name's Arthur Tribe."

"I'm William Smith."

"A visitor here?" It was evident but Tribe asked it courteously. They had fallen into step towards Lexleigh. The bitch trotted behind, sparing her nearside hind leg. Willy noticed it and asked:

"She's a little lame?"

"Good gracious, no. They all do that on one side or the other." Willy's glasses were still on the string round his neck and Tribe gave them a respectful glance. "Those are very fine glasses. Zeiss, I fancy."

"The real thing from East Germany."

"You're lucky. I would guess that you use them for watching birds."

"Birds and other things. Such as Sokenhoe."

"You're interested in Sokenhoe?"

"I'm interested in the smell of decay."

"Sokenhoe has that all right. It was once a modestly prosperous place – cabotage and the local fishing. Now the coastal trade has gone completely and the so-called local fish is caught elsewhere. All that remains is an occasional barge – bulbs from the Low Countries, a trickle of trade. The only thing left of interest at Sokenhoe is that old Martello tower behind it."

"I noticed it. I'd never seen one."

"There are a few left standing in Kent and Sussex but on this coast they're as thick as currants in a good bun."

"They were built to keep out Napoleon?"

"Right." Arthur Tribe considered before he went on. "And the military theory behind them was orthodox: you couldn't advance with any safety leaving an unreduced fortress behind you. The idea was resurrected in the last war. Strongboxes, they called them, and they turned out to be mantraps. Armour drove past them without troubling to engage them and later they were destroyed from the air." Tribe smiled wryly. "I know because I was in one myself."

"So they haven't any use today?"

"None. They're picturesque but a bit of a nuisance. The one you saw is actively dangerous – anything like a gale would bring it down. The Department which owns it would like to demolish it but the environmentalists are up in arms. The usual bureaucratic battle. Meanwhile if you go to Sokenhoe keep clear of it."

"I was thinking of going tomorrow."

"It's a long way round by road and a boring drive."

"I was thinking of walking – using the bridleway. I was looking from the Mount this morning and there's a sort of Bailey bridge across the creek."

43

"A good idea if you have the legs."

"I have the legs but I don't think I'll test the idea."

"Whyever not?"

Willy was liking this new acquaintance. He was solid and he could pass information. "Because when I went up that Mount this morning I was stopped by a man with a shotgun and ordered down here."

"I've never heard of that before. Did this man give a reason?"

"He said they were trying to close that right of way."

"What 'they'?"

"He didn't say."

"The people who own the land up there are a farming company over at Colchester. I've heard it's really owned by Arabs. But they know the locals inside out who are as stubborn as the Prophet's mule. They'd defend a right of way with their lives or at any rate up to the House of Lords. I belong to the local club at Lexleigh and I haven't heard a word of this. If anything of the sort were happening it couldn't be going on in secret. That club of mine would be talking of nothing else." Tribe shook his head. "It's very odd. And that shotgun he was carrying. Why?"

"He did give a reason for that."

"What was it?"

"He said he was also guarding the crop. Starving geese would strip that rape in a couple of hours."

Tribe shook his head again. "Utter rubbish. Pigeons might take it if the weather were hard enough but we're not much pestered by pigeons here. Pigeons like trees and woods." He waved an arm at the bare country round them. "And woods are rather a rarity here. But I've been retired here eight years without seeing a goose. There are duck on the flats round the creek at Sokenhoe – you probably picked them up in your glasses – but geese would be a nine days' wonder. Everyone with permission to shoot, and I happen to be one myself, would be fighting for one of those hides on the Mount."

44

They had walked on for perhaps a hundred yards. Tribe had been thinking and now asked diffidently: "I suppose you're not in Customs?"

"Why do you ask?"

"I was in government service myself, you know, where I picked up a nose for what wasn't what it seemed to be. I'm a retired prison governor. That sounds a bit grand but in fact was not. I was only a sort of superior screw but being one you do get perceptive."

"I believe you," Willy said.

"I'll not ask again who you are or what you do. That was a little rude. I apologise. But I'd like to ask another question."

"Go ahead. I may not answer."

"When you were up on the Mount with those glasses was there a barge tied up in Sokenhoe?"

"There was."

"I thank you."

Willy had been carefully trained and he knew when a further question would recoil; he didn't say: "Why do you ask?" but waited for Tribe's next move. It came.

"I've recently had to give up golf."

Willy Smith played this game too, the innocent statement apparently meaningless but which passed a very definite message to a listener alert to receive it. This man would talk again in his own time. "I'm staying at the Clarence," Willy said.

"I take the occasional drink at the Clarence."

They had reached the end of the dyke and the golf course. The clubhouse looked too big for Lexleigh but in the season would no doubt be crowded. "Au revoir, then," Willy said.

"Au revoir."

Tribe walked away with the dog at his heels. Once out of earshot of Willy he laughed. It hadn't been his business to say so but he was sure that the man on the Mount had been Wellworthy. He hadn't known that he guarded his cargoes and the fact that he did so was distinctly disturbing. A few

45

thousand pounds'-worth of drink or tobacco was something which might just be tolerated since there wasn't the manpower to stop it effectively but if Wellworthy grew over-ambitious, changed his merchandise to something more serious, he'd soon be in very grave trouble indeed.

In fact he was in that trouble already though not from Her Majesty's Customs and Excise.

There was a taxi setting down at the clubhouse and Willy told it to take him to the restaurant which his wife had named. The diversion the long way round by the dyke had made him twenty minutes late and he hated to keep Amanda waiting. She could be decidedly brisk when he sometimes did so but he found her contentedly drinking gin. She had guessed that he was on a job and jobs could not be timed to suit housewives.

Willy didn't drink a lot but looked enviously at her gin and tonic. "Have I time for one of those myself?"

"Of course you have. They've brought me some olives."

They were in an alcove away from the main press of the restaurant which was crowded and a little noisy. They could talk in peace and Willy began to. He did so with a total confidence and the confidence stood on two very firm grounds. First Amanda had security clearance – not in the formal sense of Whitehall but a more difficult crown which she'd won from the Colonel himself. The then head of the Security Executive had been on social terms with Amanda and Willy, sometimes dining with them formally and sometimes dropping in for pot-luck. He knew that on either occasion he would eat well. And once when it had been pot-luck Willy had been called away. It had been the moment for a necessary exchange since the wife of any operator could support or ruin his progress equally.

. . . Why hadn't she gone up to Oxbridge? She had three good As, one at scholarship level. She would have walked it.

She had answered with a becoming candour. She hadn't gone up to Oxford or Cambridge because she hadn't

46

fancied the smell of either. Undergraduates as a body bored her stiff. The males were mend-the-world-in-a-nighters and the females whined incessantly about conditions and their scant allowances. And she'd probably get laid by some curious don. Amanda had wanted none of these things.

. . . What had she wanted, then?

What she'd got. A home and a couple of children. A man. They'd been alone and the Colonel of an age she could trust. Particularly the man, she had said.

Next morning the Colonel had summoned Willy. If he wished to talk to his wife of his work he could.

That was one reason why Willy now did so. The other was more personal but to Willy Smith at least as important. For he greatly respected Amanda's intelligence. She had a better academic record than his and something which he valued more: she had flair, intuition, instinct. The word didn't matter, the gift surely did. She wasn't subject to arbitrary rules of male logic but she could see through brick walls with uncanny accuracy.

So he told her the morning's events in order. She listened without interruption – another gift. Most women began the questions too soon. The man lost the thread and got tangled in trifles.

They had eaten their way through a generous meal since both of them had excellent appetites. They were onto their coffee before he'd quite finished. Willy lit her cigarette and she said: "So you go up a hill and peek at Sokenhoe through fieldglasses. A man shoos you off with a cock and bull story about trying to close a right of way. He also has a gun for emphasis."

He nodded again.

"Pretty tight security, wasn't it? For Hassall's load of cigarettes and cheap brandy." Amanda permitted a rare irrelevance. "I like Mark Hassall but I think he's dangerous. He has some very unfashionable ideas."

"The load might have been bigger than usual. People have been known to get greedy."

"Or it might have been something else which Hassall fears?"

"There was a barge tied up at the jetty in Sokenhoe. I'll have to take a look tomorrow."

"Be careful," she said.

"I always am."

In the event he did not go for several days. It had started to snow without sign of a let-up, the heaviest fall for many years. The side roads weren't gritted and the fierce wind piled the drifts waist-high. Sokenhoe was entirely cut off except by the footpath and that was patrolled.

The interval gave Marcos time to act.

4

Harry Wellworthy had known for a year that his business was sliding into irreversible bankruptcy but had somehow persuaded himself that it was not. Now an incident had brought him face to face with the brutal fact.

It had been a small thing in its way but fatal – fatal to Wellworthy's standing locally. He was thought of as a man of substance, well considered in Lexleigh's business club, envied by others who believed he was wealthy. And he'd been refused a new car on hire purchase. Flatly. He drove a solid but aging Rover, a car appropriate to his apparent position, but when he'd sent it in for its annual test he'd been told that what was needed to put it back on the road was more than the machine was worth . . . Then what about a new one? Certainly, Mr. Wellworthy. Certainly.

Much less certainly when he'd spoken of terms. Finally the firm refusal. He couldn't go to his bank for they were pressing already on an overdraft he'd little hope of re-paying. Moreover there was the question of face. The affair would be all over town in a week. In a community like Lexleigh-on-Sea that sort of thing would leak at once.

In the mountain of his increasing troubles a new car had been in a sense a trifle but it was immediate and a good deal closer than steadily more alarming balance sheets; it brought him with a bang to reality. He must go and see his accountants at once. They had been warning him for some time but he had stalled. Now he must grasp the nettle.

If he could.

They were a well-established London firm and a Barlow had dealt with Wellworthy's grandfather. Both concerns were family businesses and Harry had dealt with that

Barlow's grandson. Now he had retired to Bournemouth and Harry wondered who would receive him in his place.

He was surprised to find a cool young woman to whom he took an instant dislike. He couldn't have given a valid reason but he was conscious that the feeling was mutual.

In fact what Patricia Spence felt for Wellworthy was rather contempt than an honest dislike. She had taken his case with open reluctance since before he had left for his villa in Bournemouth Barlow had given her careful briefing. Wellworthy's could hardly be salvaged and Harry himself had once been in prison. Patricia had not objected to that, indeed was in no position to do so since she was living with an ex-convict herself. He was a Cypriot Greek now living in England and accomplished in all matters of venery. She was wholly without what was called social conscience and was inclined to sympathise with the criminal ethos. In a real sense they were the only free men. Much of her time was spent on tax work, the no man's land between avoidance and evasion. Criminals didn't bother with that. They simply took.

So her contempt for Harry Wellworthy had nothing to do with what Barlow had told her before he left. It was a common sort of case, he had said, the vigorous acquisitive grandfather, then the genes sapped by a generation of ease till you came to a man like Harry Wellworthy, not evil but simply weak and feckless. Luckily he had a little money beside what the firm earned or rather didn't and a Calvinist wife who kept him fairly straight.

(Or did she? Barlow had secretly wondered. He too had heard gossip of small-time smuggling.)

Patricia Spence didn't care for weaklings; she liked her men hot and strong like her coffee. Like Marcos she thought with a private smile.

She took Wellworthy through the facts remorselessly. The only way to resuscitate Wellworthy's was to do what competitors had done already – turn the business of selling by glossy catalogue into garden centres with all the amenities, places where people could take the children. Playground and hot tea and coffee. Awful food.

"And where do we get the capital?"

"You tell me."

He had watched her as she talked on smoothly, disliking her the more as she did so. She was severely dressed as became her profession but she was sleek as a cat, every bit as feline.

"I've still got the house," he had said.

She had laughed. The sound had been entirely genuine but had cut him more deeply than anything forced. She really thought the remark amusing.

She said what Arthur Tribe had once thought: the house was an enormous white elephant. If it had had anything like a decent garden it might have sold well to an eager developer but as it stood it wouldn't tempt a sane one. To turn it into flats would need capital, capital which he didn't have, and in any case converted flats were difficult to sell in Lexleigh. And when he talked of selling the house how much did he owe the bank?

A lot.

She had sat back in her chair and he'd read her thoughts. This was just another hopeless case.

"Then what do you advise?"

There was no pleasure in crushing a worm and she hesitated; finally she said: "You must sell. Sell what's left of the business and try to live on the proceeds."

"Have you anyone in mind?"

"But it's obvious. The only people interested in buying up what's left of Wellworthy's would be people in the same line of business."

"A competitor, you mean?"

She nodded.

"But I couldn't do that."

"Whyever not?"

"We've been going for over a hundred years."

She was irritated but successfuly hid it. Family *pietas*, family pride, were emotions which she didn't share. She

51

had come from very little herself and the words increased her contempt for her client. "It's up to you," she said indifferently.

"I'll think it over."

"Yes, you do that."

He rose and took his leave politely but he didn't invite her to share his luncheon. For one thing he had begun to detest her and for another he couldn't afford to do so.

Patricia Spence returned to the work on her desk. She always worked fast but today she worked faster for she intended to leave at five o'clock. That was early for a successful accountant but she had reason to look her best and that took time. She was dining with her lover Marcos.

They had been together for several years but one of the things she liked about Marcos apart from his undoubted skills was that he always took enormous trouble. He treated every one of their meetings as a seduction in the grandest manner, the champagne and the caviar, the candles, later the music she loved, Puccini. Patricia could take this diet indefinitely. She knew that there were censorious persons, mostly women of progressive views, who'd have only one word for these splendid occasions. That word would be dismissive: vulgar. Patricia Spence dissented strongly. Corny, perhaps – she'd concede they were that – but what was wrong with good old corn? In whatever form of art it be good corn beat the intellectuals into the ground.

Marcos had an impressive old house in an unfashionable district of London and Cypriot servants to serve his needs. Tonight he had in no way failed her. There'd been the usual orchid (now that *was* a bit vulgar) the wine and the sort of food which he knew she liked best. It was sole with a plain butter sauce and banana and afterwards breast of chicken *à la Kiev*. Marcos himself preferred something more solid but he didn't invite Patricia for the food.

Over the meal they had talked of trifles, of politics where their views were identical. The world as it stood and the West in particular was a shambles in imminent danger of falling apart. Left and Right were distasteful in equal measure and behind all the talk stood a grinning skull. One horror bred another inevitably: the old gods would have the final laugh. So the sensible, civilised man dug his garden. That garden contained five active senses and all of them needed different nursing.

The manservant served the coffee and bowed. "Good night, sir."

"Good night, Demetrios."

They moved to armchairs and a decanter of brandy and Patricia began to talk of her day. She knew that he liked to hear her gossip. It wasn't something which he affected to please her; he was genuinely interested in other people's lives. She told him the story of Harry Wellworthy withholding only her client's name. She could see that his interest was in more than the story for she knew him well and could read him freely. Marcos was smelling a possible deal. At the end he asked simply: "So what's this man's name?"

"You know I couldn't tell you that."

"Unprofessional?"

"Yes, very."

He knew better than to press her there and then. Instead he went to the hi-fi and turned it on. He knew her tastes and honestly shared them; he liked opera but it had to be grand with a capital G. Mozartian flutings at Glyndebourne left him cold. Like coffee or a woman in bed it had to be straight and uninhibited.

It was Nilsson singing *In Questa Reggia* and they listened in increasing excitement. Patricia heard the matchless voice, Marcos the superb technique. Only a great soprano risked this one, the challenging leaps through the high *tessitura*, from middle register to the As and Bs, and that single stunning C *in alt*. A lifetime of sweat and tears to achieve it and the bloody woman made it sound easy.

At the end he saw that Patricia was trembling. He took her hand and led her upstairs.

A pert maid served them breakfast next morning. Neither ate an English one, he because he didn't like them, she because she watched her weight. But there was coffee and fresh croissants and fruit. She was as relaxed as a cat which had just been fed; she said: "You put me on the spot last night."

"I didn't mean to. What particular spot?"

"When you asked me for a client's name."

"You put me down on that one. Hard."

"And I've been wondering whether I got it right. To give a client's name is improper but to withhold it might be to deny an advantage. I don't think a lot of this client, he's wet, but he's also in very serious trouble. I've a soft spot for the lame ducks, you know."

"You shouldn't have. It doesn't pay."

"I could see you were interested."

"You see too much for a mere male's comfort. I didn't say I was interested – I don't say it now. What I do say is that there might be an opening."

Another thing she liked in Marcos was that he chose his words with care and precision. English wasn't his mother tongue but he used it with a proper respect. "An opening which my client would gain from?"

"Most openings have two ends. You know that well."

"Then my client's name is Harry Wellworthy and may nobody ever discover I told you."

Normally he moved neatly and quickly but now he made a clatter with his cup. "Harry Wellworthy? I knew him in prison."

"I didn't know that."

"There's no reason you should – he wasn't worth a discussion. He was a prison creep, always moaning to the chief screw. Some said he was also a stool. I don't know. But he wasn't a good man to have in gaol."

"So you who were a local baron took it out of the poor bastard hard."

He said coolly: "It depends what you mean – this isn't America. Knocking a man about is quite difficult but there are ways of making his life disagreeable."

"Which from time to time you took?"

"I and others."

"Then he's hardly likely to trust you in business."
She looked at her watch. "I have an appointment at
nine."

It was a fact that she had an important engagement.
There was an offshore fund which had slipped off the rails.
That was primarily meat for a lawyer but Patricia would
have an interest too and Barlow's had a tame cat solicitor.
It would have been slanderous to have called him bent but
he knew every trick in the sleazy world where the taxman
fought the taxpayer grimly. "I must go," she said.

"No, don't do that." He looked at his watch in turn and
laughed. "It is now twenty-five to nine precisely. From this
minute I'll pay standard rates for your time."

It was the sort of cynical joke she relished. "Very well,"
she said. "I'll ring the office."

"I'll do that for you." He picked up the house phone and
spoke to Demetrios. She didn't understand what was said
since she didn't know a word of Greek. But he put the
phone down and said: "All arranged. Now where were
we?"

"You were making life disagreeable for Wellworthy and
I was saying he wouldn't deal with you."

"You were wrong," he said.

"Tell me why."

"With pleasure." He poured her another coffee and
went on. "From what you tell me of Harry Wellworthy and
what I happen to hear on the network he is now a highly
respected citizen. He has a drab of a wife who tries to keep
him that way. What she doesn't know is that she hasn't
succeeded. Harry is now a small-time smuggler."

Marcos wasn't a man who made foolish statements and
she didn't waste time in querying this one. But she asked a
single legitimate question. "How do you know?"

He said with the first hint of irritation: "You may not
understand but I'll tell you. Once you've been in a prison
for over a year then in a sense you're there for the rest of
your life. People you knew and probably liked turn up and
ask for help. You give them a bit and in turn they talk,

including talk of men who were not your friends. It's a world apart and you never escape from it."

She knew that he hadn't nor even had tried to. On the contrary he'd stayed in and flourished. He had a legitimate business which served as his cover – she had met him doing that firm's accounts – but its profits didn't pay for the way he lived. As for that she had guessed he was something pretty big. He wouldn't be going out on jobs, he'd be standing behind them, finding the money and anything special.

And taking a pretty good share of the profits.

Patricia Spence smiled; she didn't object. She was totally unburdened by conscience.

He rose and escorted her down to his car. Demetrios was driving it and he got down and opened the door with a flourish. On the seat was a bunch of a dozen red roses. It was a part of Marcos's act and she loved it.

He shook hands formally with his professional adviser. He never kissed her unless he meant serious business. She liked that too.

Willy Smith had intended to visit Sokenhoe before telephoning to Mark Hassall in London but now Sokenhoe was cut off by road. The bridleway and the bridge might be passable but only to a man used to snow. Willy Smith hated snow and he knew of no urgency. Just the same he would have to ring Hassall.

He told him of his first reconnaissance and of how he'd been stopped on the Mount and turned off it. "By a man with a very tall story," he added.

"Curious," Hassall said.

"My local friend thought so too. So did I."

"Do you think that's enough to identify Sokenhoe as the place where the smuggled stuff comes in?"

"Not identify but it's something to work on. There are half a dozen places like Sokenhoe and I started there because it was nearest. All I'm going to say about Sokenhoe is that Peeping Toms are strongly discouraged."

"And the discourager – the man with the gun and the story which didn't fit? Would you recognise a photograph?"

"No. He wore nondescript clothes with a cap and a scarf. He was rough and rude but his speech was not."

There was a pause while Hassall thought; then tentatively: "Wellworthy?"

"Perhaps."

"Or someone he hired for the job?"

"Rushing it a little, aren't you?"

"You said you saw a barge at the jetty."

"A Belgian-registered barge. I saw the flag."

"And a man with a gun."

"Perhaps Wellworthy's getting over-ambitious."

"I take the point." Hassall changed the subject. "What's the weather like at Lexleigh-on-Sea?"

"Snowing to beat Siberia. Half a gale."

"So you can't get over to Sokenhoe?"

"Not unless I fly, I can't."

There was another pause before Hassall said: "That gives me an idea."

"It does?"

"The first sign of a break in this damnable weather I'll put a helicopter up over Sokenhoe. Photographs and a general look-see."

Willy said but without enthusiasm: "I agree it is an idea."

Mark Hassall was annoyed and snapped. "Have you a better?"

"None whatever."

"Of course you haven't, our hands are tied. In any other country but England I'd pull Wellworthy in and grill him brown. In any other country but England . . ."

Willy listened for a moment and then cut in. Mark Hassall had a standard piece about the iniquity of the law in England, how it weighted the balance against the police. Willy had heard it before and was bored by it. Privately he was inclined to agree but you had to take the system as it was. "I know," he said soothingly. "Put up your chopper."

Wellworthy, Willy thought as he took his bath. There was a terrible cloud of smoke about Wellworthy but his instinct was that behind it stood someone else.

When Patricia had left after breakfast Marcos went down to his study and disciplined thought. He would have confessed that he was seriously interested: two sides of a story had meshed in neatly. On the one hand he kept in touch with the grapevine and it had whispered that a man was smuggling. Petty stuff, Marcos gathered, the traditional things. His bulbs were lorried down from Holland and shipped from a Belgian port to Sokenhoe. That was cheaper than using a major port and less vulnerable to some trade union's whim. And on the other Patricia had told her tale of a man whose business was near to collapse.

And the two men were the same, Harry Wellworthy.

Marcos drew in his breath in increasing excitement. The situation was a gift from the gods, he might have planned the whole set-up himself . . . An established line of trade into Sokenhoe which couldn't be watched as closely as a big port. And that line ran from Belgium where Marcos had a powerful friend – Belgium where security was notoriously lax, where a good man could steal what he couldn't in England.

Marcos had two propositions before him. He thought of the first as conventional crime. It was going to be big, very big indeed, but politics would not come into it. In the second they would and he hadn't committed himself. He would think about that when the other was in the bag.

He was convinced that he could put it there. It would need modern arms to assure success but he knew that his friend in Belgium could steal them. Thereafter he'd run them in through Sokenhoe.

And he needn't deal with Wellworthy, or not yet; he needn't part with a single penny. Later he might have to talk to him if his second proposition was on the cards but for the moment he needn't pay. He'd take. A single run from Belgium would do it and he needn't choose one

58

of Wellworthy's barges. Nor would he be paying freight. What he wanted could be slipped aboard easily and a couple of men to highjack the ship at sea. Other birds had a lot to learn from the cuckoo.

Quickly, then, but his gods were with him. He would need two days to make his arrangements, before anybody could interfere, but his gods had sent him convenient snow.

He called the weather bureau to confirm his luck. Yes, most of East Anglia was impassable and getting worse. In a couple of days, perhaps, but hardly before . . .

Marcos rang his friend in Belgium.

The barge which had brought in Wellworthy's cargo had slipped away as the snowstorm blew itself out. The chopper arrived just in time to see her and saw something else at least as interesting. Another craft was nosing in, bigger than a barge, a small tramp. "Belgian flag again," the pilot said.

"It would be. But we'll do Sokenhoe first and take a look at her later."

They flew low over Sokenhoe, taking their photographs. "What a hole," the observer said.

"It's a dump."

Their photographs finished they circled the tramp. "She'll have to be careful to get in and out. She'll have to judge the tides to an inch."

Her captain had thought so too but he didn't now care. He was lying gagged and trussed in the hold. There'd been himself and a hand and the boy who cooked. Normally he took only bulk cargo but this time there'd been a couple of crates. And halfway across the Channel they'd jumped him, two men he had never seen, with guns. The hand and the boy they had coldly shot and they were lying beside him now in the hold.

He wondered why they had left him alive. Presumably, he decided, as hostage. If something went wrong he might conceivably be useful but if it didn't he was surely dead.

These men would land whatever they'd brought with them. And then? Then they wouldn't dare take the ship back to Belgium so they'd put out to sea and somewhere scuttle her. There was an inflatable with an outboard motor and that they would use to reach land themselves. Where no doubt they'd have friends who would take them over. Whatever this operation be it had been carefully planned and had accepted large risks. You didn't shoot men down in cold blood if you were running brandy or even hash.

The captain heard the chopper's clatter and for the third time hopelessly fought his bonds. Then the noise of the rotor faded and he lay still. He commended his soul to God and tried to sleep.

5

Harry Wellworthy woke next morning alert and refreshed. He had slept nine hours like a baby without a care, or rather without an immediate care, and he had trained himself not to look further than that. Petty smuggling had brought in a little money, enough to help with the household bills, but the barge which Willy had seen through his glasses before Wellworthy had warned him away had been carrying four times the usual run. Arthur Tribe and later Willy Smith had been right in their similar speculation. Harry Wellworthy had got suddenly greedy.

He was a timid man and the decision had frightened him for he wasn't a fool and could assess probabilities. One would be that he was suspect already since there were other men necessarily involved in his set-up and he'd be unwise to rely on complete discretion. But unless one of his bargemen were caught redhanded it would be difficult to bring a case which a British court would accept and convict on. Customs were known to be stretched to their limit with the rising flood of addictive drugs and Wellworthy had always kept clear of those. Nevertheless he had been on edge till his barge had unloaded and slipped away.

Now he put any doubts behind him and savoured his luck. He had money now, ten thousand pounds, chicken feed to a major criminal but then he wasn't playing in that league. Like Marcos who had passed as a Big Boy. Well, he'd never see Marcos again, that was certain.

Ten thousand pounds – it would put him straight locally. It would do nothing to save his crumbling business but it would pay pressing bills and leave something to spare. It

61

would be pleasant to go to that garage and offer cash for a new car. That would get round at least as fast as the fact that he'd been refused hire purchase. And he could give his wife a little more housekeeping. She was grimly economical as she was dourly efficient in everything else but he knew that what he gave her was not enough. And they still had to pay that resentful old maid. Maggie wouldn't hear of dismissing her. She'd been with them for far too long. It would be wrong.

Wrong, he thought as he dressed deliberately – the word ruled Maggie's life inexorably. He knew why he had married her or rather why she had married him: he'd been a brand to be snatched from the burning, a duty. She would keep him straight if doing so killed her. It would atone in some minuscule way for Original Sin. And at first it had been more than tolerable since Maggie had known her wifely duty and she wasn't an unattractive woman. For a year they had shared a bed, then he'd left it. He had done so without regret or protest for he had seen her shut her teeth in the act of love. Now occasionally he slipped up to London.

He went downstairs and cooked her breakfast. Poor old silly, he thought, she deserved her breakfast. Breakfast in bed was her sole concession to what she knew was the mortal sin of sloth.

He took it to her and went down to his study. Maggie had always called it his den. She spoke of Men with an almost audible capital. They were different animals who must be treated accordingly and one of their perks was a room of their own. So Harry had his room of his own and once in it she would leave him alone. He would give her that. His study was sacrosanct.

He was glad that it was since they didn't communicate. In it he had his books and a telly. Maggie read too but different books, an unchanging diet of hard theology. Once he had stayed after meals to chat to her but she had only two subjects of conversation: the affairs of the house and man's hereafter. He realised that she was passing learned but religion in the abstract bored him stiff . . . For example what in hell was a Jansenist? Harry gathered he didn't think much of the human race. It was naturally evil and therefore incorrigible. To the orthodox that was an evident heresy since it flatly denied the doctrine of Grace and at first these men had been properly persecuted. Later they seemed to have made their peace and now were back under Rome's umbrella. Uneasily, perhaps, but still under it. And there was a clear but slightly dotty distinction between a Jansenist and Maggie's own Calvinist creed.

Fascinating if such stuff was your interest but if it wasn't it was a boring obsession. Meanwhile he had a little money. The immediate pressure was off. Seize the day.

Like her husband Amanda Smith was enjoying Lexleigh. Snow still held a thrill for her and she was sorry that her sons weren't there to romp in it. But the whole of southern England was covered so no doubt they'd be having their fun at school. She and her husband had chosen it carefully for there were still prep schools which took the lofty line that learning was of little importance, it was character-building which really counted. Amanda herself had done well at school and Willy had played cricket for Harrow. Neither was going to be taken in by some second-class schoolmaster prating of "character". She missed her sons but she knew they were cared for well.

It was pleasant, too, to have nothing to do. She was a better than average family cook and relished feeding Willy well but the food at the Clarence was much as she liked it and when they went out they went to Barbara's. Above all she enjoyed what she called her shopping. The shop-keepers at Lexleigh-on-Sea were polite and much more obliging than those at home. They seemed to be pleased to have your custom. Some of them would even deliver. There'd been no curious glances, no moments of a vague embarrassment. Amanda had been carriage trade and that was that.

This morning she had finished her shopping, trifles which she liked to buy leisurely, and was sitting drinking coffee in Barbara's. She had allowed herself two éclairs and one was left. She knew that they were excessively fattening but any weight she put on she could lose as easily. Her friends envied her that but she took it for granted. At this hour Barbara's wasn't crowded and a woman came in and looked round casually. She made for an empty table, then changed her mind. She walked to Amanda Smith's, asked politely: "Do you mind if I join you?"

"Of course not. Please do."

The woman looked at the éclair and permitted a smile. "You always had an excellent appetite."

"I'm sorry, I don't remember – "

"Why should you? I'm Maggie Adams, or rather I was. Now I'm Mrs. Margaret Wellworthy."

Amanda remembered Maggie Adams: she'd been a teacher at her convent school. Her own parents had been stoutly Methodist but the school had been the best in the neighbourhood and prided itself that it didn't proselytise. The atmosphere had been properly Catholic and some-times girls wished to join the Faith. The Reverend Mother gave them an interview and sometimes a glass of sherry with it . . . Come back in a couple of years, my dear. If you're still of the same mind we'll find you a priest. Amanda said: "And I'm now Mrs. Smith with two strap-ping boys."

"I envy you," Maggie Wellworthy said.

"Oh, I don't know. They're a terrible handful."

"But worth it. I have nothing. Nothing."

Amanda thought the conversation was becoming a little tense for a coffee shop but then, she remembered, Miss Maggie Adams had always been the odd woman out. In the convent there'd been the Blacks and the Browns. The Blacks had been the regular nuns and the girls had much preferred them to the Browns. The Blacks had been strict but you knew where you were with them but the Browns had been some sort of oblate and all oblates were crazy by definition. Moreover you could never quite trust them; they got up to games; they spied and sneaked. Maggie Adams had not been a Brown but a teacher, a lay teacher and, it followed, a good one for the school's academic standard had been high. It was known that she was not a Catholic but it had been whispered that she wished to convert. Apparently nothing had come of that. Amanda said lightly to cool it down: "And when did you leave St. Anne's?"

"Four years ago. I was hoping to become a Black." She smiled. "I'd never have looked at those dreadful Browns – I disliked them as much as I know the girls did. It was all or nothing for me, you know, and nothing was what I finally got."

Amanda was getting dangerously interested. Against her better judgement she asked: "The Blacks turned you down?"

"They turned me down flat." She added with apparent irrelevance. "I'm a daughter of the Manse, you know."

Amanda understood her at once. This was nothing to do with religion whatever but the Blacks had been mostly Anglo-Irish, ladies of established families and under their sober liveries still conscious of class . . . A daughter of the Manse, my dear? Well . . . Well . . .

"So what did you do then?"

"I left. For a couple of years I taught elsewhere then I married a man I wasn't in love with."

"I hear that sometimes works rather well. You neither of you expect too much."

"It didn't work with me."

"I'm sorry."

Amanda decided to shut this down: it was getting too hot and altogether too intimate. She called for her bill but changed her mind suddenly. This woman had been an excellent teacher and Amanda owed her one of her excellent As. She was clearly under stress and miserable. It would be ungrateful as well as ungracious to cut her short.

Amanda Smith ordered two more coffees, offering an éclair which was declined. She put away her own, then said tentatively: "I'm sorry about the no children."

"So am I. But it isn't only that."

Astonished to hear her own voice Amanda said: "You'd better tell me."

There was a silence while Margaret Wellworthy thought. Amanda realised that she was eager to talk. Calvinists didn't think much of Confession but like everyone else they felt its need. Finally Margaret Wellworthy spoke.

"I suppose you're not a policewoman."

"Certainly not."

"Nor your husband a policeman?"

"No."

"I ask because women talk to their husbands, or at any rate the happy ones do. It's a waste of breath to ask them not to."

"You're observant," Amanda said.

"I have to be." Another and rather longer silence. At last it came out in a sort of despair. "My husband is doing something wicked."

"Wicked," Amanda thought – what a word! Anyone else would have said "shifty" or even "criminal". For a moment she was genuinely sorry for whoever had married Margaret Adams. But she said: "How wicked?"

"I'm afraid very wicked."

"Slips up to London sometimes, does he?"

"Not very often. It's worse than that."

Amanda Smith was losing patience. She owed this woman a hearing but not all day. "Out with it," she said crisply. "Tell."

Maggie Wellworthy drew a long breath and discharged it. "He's breaking the law."

"What law?"

"I can't tell you that."

"Of course you can't. I apologise. A stupid question."

"In any case I don't *know*. But I'm sure."

66

It was the sort of statement which Margaret Adams, good teacher, would never have made to an intelligent pupil. She seemed to realise it for she added suddenly: "My husband has been in prison, you see."

"Did you know that when you married him?"

"Yes. It was really the reason I married him at all."

"I don't think I follow that."

"I couldn't expect you would. You see – " She broke off with a gesture of faint disgust; she had used the feeble words unthinkingly and they offended a good teacher's nicety. Of course the banality was self-excusing; she wouldn't have used it if she hadn't unconsciously felt that she must. But Amanda's steady eyes were still on her. She finished the last of her coffee and said: "I felt it was a sort of duty. A sort of, well, a sort of Grace. I'd keep him straight if it killed me. And I've failed. But I can't expect you to understand."

"Oddly enough I'm half way to doing it. I'm Methodist myself as you know and Methodists aren't much given to mysticism. But I know it when I see it in front of me."

On a note which came very close to offence Margaret Wellworthy said: "So you think I'm a mystic?"

"There is more than one kind of mystic, you know."

"None is to my taste." Margaret Wellworthy rose unexpectedly. She'd heard something she hadn't expected to hear, not the easy words of comfort she'd longed for but a challenge to search her own conscience again. "You've been very kind," she said. "Goodbye."

Amanda related the morning's talk to her husband at lunch. She had expected an intelligent interest but not the open excitement Willy showed. "Now that," he said, "is really something."

"The woman's story, you mean?"

"No. Her name."

"I don't get that."

"So I'll try to explain. You remember I told you I was here on a job." He gave her an affectionate smile. "Not that you hadn't already guessed it. And I told you that job was connected with smuggling. Petty smuggling but Hassall gave me a name. That name was Mr. Harry Wellworthy.''

Amanda said unhappily: ''So now you're going to go after Wellworthy.''

He laughed. ''Extremely improbable. I'm not interested in petty smuggling; nor is Mark. What he fears is something a whole lot more dangerous, something that might be a political crime which would bring in the Executive at the run. That's why I'm here.''

''Political crime sounds well outside Wellworthy's form.''

''I get tired of saying you're a very bright girl. But Wellworthy has an established smuggling line, Wellworthy might get taken over. Just between the two of us I've a hunch it's been taken over already.''

''Anything to go on?''

''Nothing.''

''And Mark?''

''The usual stirrings of dust in squalid corridors. That's how the police sometimes get in first.''

''And the Executive?''

''One stage removed but properly scared. We're paid to deal with political crime which means preventing it if we can get there ahead of it.''

''What are you going to do?''

''Now the snow's stopped I'm going over to Sokenhoe. But I'll have to ring Mark first and clear the line.''

He did so at Mark Hassall's home since he suspected that he had exceeded his powers in enlisting the Executive privately and he might not wish to be over-heard by others who would at least be curious. He had risen fast to his present rank but Willy knew that there were senior officers who regarded him as, well, not quite safe. Nor was he – that was why he was good. He would cut corners and he would take a risk. Such as suggesting a visit to Lexleigh by Willy on a guess that what seemed to be petty smuggling might soon involve something much more dangerous, something political and therefore the Executive's meat. It had been the action of a far-sighted official but not one of a wholly orthodox police-man.

Hassall listened in silence and then said shortly: "It's confirmatory about Wellworthy but I think the spotlight's moved on from Wellworthy."

"So?"

"You remember I put up that chopper at Sokenhoe? Its shots of the place told us nothing special but it did see something else of interest. There was a ship working in to the Sokenhoe creek and she wasn't one of Wellworthy's barges. Moreover she was registered at Blankenberg which isn't the port Wellworthy uses for his bulbs and whatever else he dabbles in."

"What sort of ship was she?"

"A small coastal tramp."

"Will she be there still?"

"By the table of tides she'll have to be there. She could only get in or out at high tide and the next one is at ten tomorrow."

"Giving her time to discharge?"

"I'm afraid so."

Willy was silent, not asking the questions. There was all night to act but insurmountable difficulties. Hassall could get men to Sokenhoe quickly but they'd be men without any formal authority, without a warrant to search or good cause to detain, men in what was a policeman's nightmare. In their own field Customs had some very strange powers and Hassall's job was to liaise with them closely but they would want something more than a policeman's suspicion before putting their machine into gear. And it would take them some time to mount an effective raid. Willy Smith said but without conviction: "You could put up that chopper again."

"What for? A chopper flying about by day could be there

for one of a dozen reasons but put her over a haven at night, coming down low and dropping flares, and it'd be obvious to the thickest seaman that something was wrong. If his cargo were in the least suspicious he'd keep it in his hold and wait for the tide. Then he'd slip out to sea and do one of two things: either he'd give up and go home or maybe he'd try somewhere else." Willy could almost see Hassall shake his head. "Which is the last thing we can afford to happen. There are other decaying harbours than Sokenhoe or at a pinch you could land by boat on a beach. No, so long as we know it's Sokenhoe, so long as one end of the line is identified, we have something to work on for what it's worth. But throw the whole position open . . ."

Hassall left it at that and Willy thought. It seemed a very long time since Mark had approached him, talking of Marcos who financed big crime. So far it had been orthodox crime, money the motive and money the spoils. But there had been whispers of something which wasn't for money, some political outrage which had made Willy shiver. Hassall had spoken of a second opinion but in fact he'd been giving a friendly warning. And anything political would be very much the Executive's business. Willy said: "Let's get this straight. That tramp steamer was spotted yesterday evening?"

"An hour after the snow stopped."

"Right. And she was working in on the evening tide?"

"So the chopper reported."

"And you think she can't get out till the next tide tomorrow. At ten."

"I mess about in boats. I know she can't."

"I can get to Sokenhoe before ten tomorrow."

"You can?" He sounded both relieved and grateful.

"I'd have been there before if the weather had let me. It didn't but now it's more or less normal."

"But that would have been a sort of reconnaissance into territory presumably open. Now it isn't open but very much occupied. By an unknown ship with an unknown cargo. And totally unknown intentions."

"I can't help that. I'll have to go."

"Good luck," Mark Hassall said.

"I may need it."

6

Willy took the car next morning, smiling tolerantly as he opened the door. It was a biggish family five-door Estate and was treated as a family tool. Neither Willy nor Amanda Smith cared a fig for a car as a symbol of status and this one needed a wash rather badly. Amanda treated it as a cupboard on wheels and the back was piled with assorted oddments, tennis racquets, the children's swimming gear, packed lunches which hadn't been eaten, old shoes. When washed and polished, which happened infrequently, the car looked rather better than average. This morning it looked like a sluttish servant.

Willy began to drive it carefully. The thaw was not yet complete or final and there was still snow under the hedges and in the fields. But the roads were slush and it hadn't refrozen. Sokenhoe which he'd seen through his glasses, perhaps half a mile distant beyond its creek, was a good twelve miles by an uninteresting route. Willy drove slowly, picking the scent up. There were patches of roadside ribbon development, bungalows and wooden chalets. Behind them was sour-looking farm land, the occasional farmhouse in need of paint. Such people as he saw were elderly, gulls wheeled over the fields mewing sadly. This countryside wasn't quite dead but was dying.

He found the turning which would take him to Sokenhoe, using his map since there wasn't a sign-post. The track was rutted and Willy drove carefully, watching the creek to his left as it broadened towards the sea. At low tide it would be a ditch between mud-flats but at the moment the tide was almost high.

Willy drove round two bends and saw Sokenhoe. On

a reflex he suppressed a shiver. This wasn't a question of dying. It was death.

He locked the car and began to explore. History was written large in decay. This had once been a prosperous thriving haven, its population perhaps five or six hundred. Now the cottages were in ruins or shuttered. There was an inn but its sign had gone. It was shut. Along the waterfront was a line of warehouses, most of them crumbling but one still in use. The board along its front read WELLWORTHY and below was a faded Royal Warrant looking ashamed. Willy looked at the door. It was firmly padlocked. Behind what was left of what had once been the village he could see the Martello tower in its nakedness. A stranger – now what was his name? Yes, Tribe – had told him that it was unsafe. If it was it was not unique in this eerie place.

Willy turned to the quay behind him and stared. Two old men were sitting on bollards, incurious. He knew they were alive since both smoked pipes but neither got up from his bollard nor hailed him. Life seemed to have drained away from them as it had from what had once been Sokenhoe.

But one sign of it remained, the tramp steamer. Her stern was tied to the rotting jetty, her bow pointing towards the open sea. At low tide she'd be on the mud and helpless but for twenty minutes more she'd have water. Willy knew little of ships and tides but the creek was much too narrow to turn in so she must have nosed in stern first. Quite a feat. Whoever was her captain knew his job.

He knew his job but by now was unconscious.

Willy walked along the jetty cautiously, avoiding the planks which looked most rotten. The tramp's little bridge was facing away from him but there was a man on her deck in a wooden chair. The galley chimney was smoking comfortably. There was a strong smell of frying sausage and cabbage. Willy hailed the man in the chair.

"Good morning."

"*Morge.*" The accent was littoral Flemish and terrible, as

coarse as the sausages frying below. A Dutchman would
have been much offended but Willy who knew no Dutch
was indifferent.

"Putting out to sea?" he enquired.

The Fleming pointed at the Belgian flag; he said labor-
iously: "I not speak Englisher."

Willy mimed a ship casting off and moving away.

"*Op den ogenblick. Rond tien.*"

Willy caught the "tien" and went on talking. There was
something about this Fleming which wasn't in part. His
manner belied his peasant speech.

"Then I think I'll have a look at that tower."

The Fleming's eyes flickered and he seemed to be thinking. He said finally in excellent English: "I wouldn't do that
if I were you."

Willy ignored the previous lie. "Why not?"

"Because it's dangerous. There's a notice to say so."

"Then I won't go too close."

"Don't go at all."

"I'm interested in old buildings, you know."

The Fleming shrugged. "On your own head be it."

"Good morning, then."

The Fleming grunted.

Willy felt his way back on the rotting jetty but once on the
quay risked a sudden movement. He turned and looked
at the tramp and the Fleming. He was speaking into a
walkie-talkie.

Willy walked through the ruined village quickly, taking
the path which led to the tower. "Tower," he was thinking,
was distinctly misleading. Towers were tall and slim and
elegant, some eighteenth-century nobleman's folly. This
building was dumpy and squat, a fort. He had heard that it
had been manned by militia, the descendants of the local
fyrd. They would have fought the French with an equal
stubbornness, men defending their own homes and fields.

He looked at the path as he walked along it. It was
muddy but had been recently used. He bent and examined
the tyre marks carefully . . . Hm, four-wheel drive, perhaps

74

a Range Rover. Maybe a small van. He couldn't be sure except that the markings were fresh and clear.

Twenty yards from the tower he stopped and inspected it. It had been built in brick and later rendered but the rendering had long since gone and was lying in piles at the base of the crumbling fort. The brickwork was visibly, dangerously rotting and in two places was cracked from top to bottom. The warning notice with skull and crossbones struck Willy as entirely unnecessary.

But the building hadn't been skimped or jerry-built. The windows which Willy guessed were embrasured, gunports if it came to a siege, were faced outside with handsome stone. Inside there would be two floors at least and probably a room for an officer. The garrison wouldn't have lived too badly for they'd have been countrymen in their own dour country, doing other things than drill and wait for the hated French. Around the tower were traces still of land which had been profitably worked, vegetables, Willy imagined, domestic stock. And the fort had one unusual feature, a parapet round the flat top, mostly fallen with the splintered rendering into untidy heaps round the tower's perimeter. As he looked at it he had an impression of movement but it was fleeting and uncertain. He put it aside.

Willy walked up to the door and looked at that. It was the original oak on enormous iron hinges secured by a bar and a grouted staple. He noticed the padlock and whistled softly. It was brand new and it was something else; it was the same make as the lock which held Wellworthy's warehouse.

He stepped back for a final look before leaving and a piece of the parapet crashed down where he'd stood. He turned his back on the tower though it cost him an effort and walked quickly back to the shabby quay. His instinct was to run but he fought it. If someone was going to shoot they'd shoot anyway.

On the quay there had been two changes since he left. The two old men still sat smoking in silence, living but in a world of ghosts, and there was activity on the coastal tramp. She had cast off and was already moving. And a smallish van had parked in a street which led to the quay. Willy could see that the crew were not in the cab.

He hesitated but went up to it firmly. It had the look of a medium-sized removal van but the name had been recently painted out. He tried to read through the fresh paint but failed.

A bullet cracked into the van to his left, two seconds later another to his right. Both had struck six inches from his head.

Willy dropped and crawled fast to a ruined cottage, dodging through the back gardens to his car. The skeletons of what had once been houses would protect him from any fire till he reached it but once off the quay on the open track he'd be the easiest mark to a competent marksman.

He climbed into his car and started it, driving off the quayside onto the track. It was far too rutted for fancy driving and Willy's pace was barely past walking. Another bullet smashed the rear window. Willy risked his suspension and total breakdown. He took the speed up to forty and held it, gritting his teeth as the car lurched dangerously. If he could reach the first of those two bends he'd be safe. A fourth bullet came through the roof but he made the bend.

He slowed but not a lot – he had business. That business was to reach Hassall quickly and once on a proper road he'd let her go.

There was a social club in Lexleigh-on-Sea which offered snooker and bowls and the daily papers. There was a bar where you could get wine or spirits but the popular drink was beer in some quantity. Arthur Tribe was a member but seldom went there for the bar was locally known as God's Waiting Room and though he'd accepted middle age he was far from an established decline. But tonight he had felt a need for company and had returned with a nagging sense of futility.

As he lit his last pipe he decided to face it: he had seldom put a foot far wrong but he had never brought off a big coup in his life. He had always done his duty – what of it? He had fought in a war, then joined a Service. In it he had risen quite high but his old-fashioned ideas had barred the top. Mental honesty – again what of it? It didn't warm a man getting older. He had recently had to give up golf since it wasn't a game he enjoyed playing badly but he came of long-lived country stock and had another fifteen years before him. When he came to the end of those and died what could he look back on with a smile? He had never done a dishonourable deed but neither had he done anything memorable, anything out of the ordinary, daring, something to warm his spirit in his grave.

Except, he remembered, that gun to Janet Clegg. He thought of it with a satisfied pride. He didn't believe in a life hereafter but if there were such a thing that would count in his favour.

. . . Janet Clegg – he had made a mess of that. He'd been cautious and sensible, everything admirable. And here he was in his early sixties, vigorous and healthy but alone.

His dog jumped into his lap and pawed him. Ordinarily that wasn't allowed, but tonight he spoke to her, scratching her ears. She could read his moods as a woman would but she wasn't the same as Janet Clegg.

He sighed and poured a considerable drink. He wouldn't be getting a second chance.

7

Willy, who had driven professionally, made excellent time towards London and Hassall but he stopped on the way to ring Amanda. She had been edgy about his visit to Sokenhoe and if he didn't return for lunch she would worry. He caught her returned from her shopping and said: "I've got to go up to London at once."

"Try not to get a dose."

"I will."

It was a private joke and a trifle threadbare but the more comfortable in the wearing for that. Willy must have a mysterious mistress, a titled lady who lived in Belgravia. She gave him the dope on a spy ring's doings and in return he dutifully paid for his supper. They had built the fantasy up together and both of them still thought it pleasing. It was also useful in lowering tension.

Amanda asked: "Has something happened?"

"The police would certainly call it an incident."

"You're not hurt?"

"I'm not hurt. I'll see you this evening and tell you all."

"Don't make it too late."

"I don't want to be late. I like my home comforts and family cooking. As for the latter we'll go to Barbara's."

He had already made a date with Mark Hassall and drove straight to his hideous glass and steel office. Hassall looked at Willy and rang a bell. "I'm breaking every rule in the book but I'm sending for a couple of drinks."

"I confess I could use one."

"So I see."

Willy sipped his drink and told his story. At the end Hassall said: "That minder was taking a risk in shooting."

"But one which he had calculated carefully. Consider.

Sokenhoe is a ghost village but one where a serious crime is brewing. From time to time there's a shop on wheels and probably a friendly vehicle with provisions for the lonely minder. He can see that my car is neither."

"Agreed."

"He's had orders to discourage the curious but there's an outside chance I'm some innocent visitor. If that's the case and he shoots up my car the police will be all over Sokenhoe in an hour."

"So he waits?"

"He waits till I behave suspiciously. I go to the barge and chat up the Captain, then I move on to the tower and case it thoroughly. A tourist might have done one but hardly both. The minder has had his suspicions – now they're confirmed."

"Then let's take the first things first. That bit of masonry which someone pushed down on you. Would it have killed you if you hadn't stepped back?"

"Probably not. I wasn't wearing a helmet but I have a pretty thick skull. Or I'm supposed to have," Willy added coolly. It was said without the least hint of resentment.

"And the first two bullets missed you narrowly. The third came through the rear window sideways and the fourth tore the roof but didn't hit you. Now what do you make of that?"

"I'll tell you. Either the man was a rotten shot or else he was an extremely good one."

"My money is on the second."

"So is mine."

"Then Sokenhoe's under tight control. Not so tight that it is permitted to kill but plenty tight enough to justify shooting. That's interesting but by no means all. Did you get that van's number?"

"No. I was being shot at."

"Quite so. In any case it was probably false. The owner's name had been painted out and you couldn't decipher what lay underneath. My bet again is that it was *Marcos Removals*. Marcos runs a removals business as cover for

79

how he makes his real money. In this case it has also been useful." Hassall put his elbows on the desk, joining his fingers together judicially. For a policeman it was an unusual gesture. "Continuing from what is known that coaster was putting to sea as you left. That means that she had already unloaded and since whatever she held wasn't lying about it had also been moved to that tower or the warehouse. Which doesn't much matter: the timing does. While you were busy driving here they've had time to load that van, probably to switch to another. Some time the first will be found abandoned, burnt out to the chassis, a job for the forensic pundits. That isn't going to help till too late. Whatever that Belgian coaster was carrying is safely cached somewhere south of Luton."

"Why not a wider area?"

"Why indeed? I'll tell you what I suspect and what I know. I suspect on what increasingly comes to us that Marcos is planning two strikes before he retires. The first is a common crime for gain and the second – why I brought you into this – is a political outrage I prefer not to think about. And now for what I really *know*." Hassall lowered his hands from their position of prayer and with one of them struck the steel desk lightly. "The next big chance of a really big crime – ordinary crime, I mean, a commercial – is in southern England and comes tomorrow. It's gold," he said, "and an awful lot of it."

"What are you going to do?"

"The usual things. Warnings in the loudest voice possible. But warnings aren't proof against modern weapons."

"And at Sokenhoe?"

"Nothing and with very good reason. I could send a man there to poke about and at the moment there's no reason to fire at him, but there'll be a minder still who'd of course be suspicious. A first man casing a rotting fort could be covered by one of several guesses, but a second could equally clearly not. And suspicion is the immediate danger, especially, I'm afraid, to you. As far as concerns what may happen tomorrow I have done what I can which is to pass information. It isn't my job to guard consignments of bullion. But if we're right in suspecting there's a bigger one brewing that's going to be your business before it's mine. And all you have to work on in practice is the knowledge that there's a line into Sokenhoe. Stir that up, create alarm and suspicion, and Marcos will simply move elsewhere. And we can't watch every creek in the land."

Willy thought this over: it made good sense. "So if you haven't enough to pull in Marcos what do I do?"

"I suggest you go back to Lexleigh and wait. Keep your head down – you're on holiday still. Above all things keep away from Sokenhoe. Once you could be some archaeologist, a second time you would smell to heaven. So keep away from Sokenhoe."

"I will."

"And if and when something happens this end I'll be on to you at once."

"Tomorrow, I think you said."

"I guessed."

Marcos had needed to make no guesses. He knew. Once that intruder had been chased away the van had been loaded, the goods delivered. He had fulfilled his side of the bargain, earned his fee. He could afford to sit back and wait in confidence.

Responsibility was something to be avoided on principle so the Departments concerned had been locked in a furious fight for some weeks to decide which should finally carry the can in the matter of moving bullion to Heathrow. The Minister responsible had taken the warnings which reached him seriously and, privately, had approached the army. But the army had learned its lessons in Ulster where whatever it did or did not had been deemed to be wrong . . . Yes, given a legitimate order it would certainly move gold from A to B but the order must be one to do a job – without strings. The army would then make its own arrangements and if these raised eyebrows in sensitive circles that would be something for politicians to defend, not Generals. One thing it would certainly not do, no sir, was to provide an escort of armed men in a truck under a junior officer who could be thrown to the wolves. There wouldn't be time for the elaborate procedure laid down in giving Aid to the Civil Power . . . We hate the sound of this job but will take it if we must. But only on the basis that we do it our own way or not at all.

So the Minister had run between office and office and had ended with the inevitable compromise. The move would be made by a private firm in the heaviest of its plated vehicles and the police would provide a respectable escort. This escort would of course be armed but it wouldn't be carrying the sort of weapons which it was rumoured an attacker might be. It neither had them nor the desire to do so. If government wanted a Heavy Protection Squad then it must authorise it and face the uproar.

In the event the attack was made with precision. The convoy was made up of three vehicles, the first a car with plain clothes police, the second the lumbering van which slowed the pace, and a third car with more police as rear-guard. And it was hit with the deadly punch of missiles. The first blew the leading police car to pieces, blocking the van and the car behind it. The second, much bigger, tore the side from the helpless van. A burst of fire killed the crew in the cab. Police ran from the rear-guard car and were mown down too.

Masked men jumped from two open trucks and looted the van. Bullion boxes were heavy to handle but they had brought a small fork-lift trolley with them. They loaded the two trucks and drove away. The fork-lift trolley they left behind them with the wreck of one police car, the dead of the second.

The raid had been rehearsed to take ninety-four seconds. In action it had taken ninety-two.

Mark Hassall rang Willy Smith that evening. "Have you heard the news?" The voice was grim.

"Only the outlines – I saw the box. What's going on behind the scenes?"

"The two trucks got clean away and have vanished. They'll be found in time burnt out like Marcos's van. The gold will have been safely hidden but nowhere near where the trucks were discovered. When the heat is off a little the bars will be melted down – recast. There's an outside chance of a slip-up there and another when it comes to selling but I don't put it high – it's been done before, on a smaller scale and with much less violence but there's a drill for disposing of stolen bullion."

"Talking of violence they threw the book at that convoy."

"Forensic is working on that for what it's worth. The rockets were American-made and can hardly have come from an active unit which would spot such a loss at once and report it. So they came from some depot or dump and there's the rub. Nobody is admitting a loss and though they'll be ordered to check their inventories that will take weeks and a cover-up's possible. Not that it matters much. Strike One had succeeded. As for Strike Two I just don't know but it's going to need something bigger than rockets. Marcos is one up and one to go. Whether he'll play the eighteenth is a guess." The voice went suddenly harsh and resentful. "Now if I were a Russian or even a Frenchman –"

"I know, I know." Willy was sympathetic and soothing but he didn't want the set piece again. "What do you want me to do meanwhile?"

"Stay on in Lexleigh, please. Keep your eyes open. I've a hunch the next development is going to be in Lexleigh-on-Sea."

"Any particular reason?"

"One. Marcos has sent a man there."

"What sort of man?"

"An unexpected one – very. He isn't a thug and he isn't an operator. He's Marcos's personal servant and has no form. His name is Demetrios and I'll try and get a photograph."

"Meanwhile if anything happens – "

83

"He's a Cypriot Greek like Marcos himself. His native language is demotic Greek but he speaks English without a trace of accent. Age somewhere in the early thirties."

Willy thought hard before finally asking: "You think I've been identified?"

"It's possible but also unlikely. Of the cast of the play which we're currently watching only Wellworthy has seen you once, a Fleming in a tramp which has gone and whoever had you cold in his sights. On the other hand Strike Two is political. Your name appears in no book of reference but the people who need to know such things will know there's a West Indian on the Board of the Executive."

"So you think this Demetrios is watching *me*?"

"I didn't say that since I couldn't prove it. But Marcos didn't send him to Lexleigh to take the air. He's there to report on something or somebody. If it's somebody then it's Willy Smith."

Marcos very seldom watched telly, considering it a waste of life. A man could eat and drink, make love, read books; he could even, if he were that sort of man, hit balls about without loss of dignity. But watching shadows was not a civilised pastime. The material was homogenised rubbish and as for the news that was painfully slanted. The slant was either Right or Left according to who was paying the piper.

So Marcos hadn't heard on the box that what Hassall had called Strike One had succeeded but he took an evening paper and he smiled as he read the flaring headline. He didn't go out on jobs himself, his business was to make them possible, but as he looked below the headline, reading on, he realised that the tools he'd imported had been used with the ruthless skill he admired. All over in under two minutes. Elegant. He had had no part in any of this but later, when the first dust had settled, he'd be approached again in the matter of cashing in, recasting the gold and finally selling it. These were matters within his

84

normal competence. There was always the chance of an unforeseen slip but Marcos didn't fear one seriously.

He smiled happily as he put down the newspaper. He'd had two propositions and the first had succeeded. He could now consider the second more carefully.

When Sheikh Sayyid had approached him first Marcos had been distinctly cool. To begin with he hadn't much cared for Sheikh Sayyid. He'd been grandiloquent in the Arab manner, talking of the Political Crime of the Twentieth Century. Marcos, a Greek, mistrusted hyperbole and Marcos, a successful criminal in a world where success was measured in money, had never considered political crime where the motive would be very different. Not that there wouldn't be money in this one too. Sheikh Sayyid had offered a million pounds and Marcos had never doubted he had it. He'd have the whole resources of a rogue State behind him. Marcos hadn't turned him down but had asked for time to think it over.

When Sheikh Sayyid had come back a week later Marcos's opinion of him had changed. For this wasn't some drug-high terrorist's fantasy but a carefully considered and feasible project. Willy Smith had been entirely wrong: the two Arabs whom he'd outfaced in the Clarence were exactly what they had claimed to be, merchants. Arabs had been buying East Anglian land and these had been casting round for more. They were the money behind the farming company which owned land around Lexleigh including the Mount; and beyond it, beyond Sokenhoe, was other run-down land which was going cheap. It would need capital to make it profitable but these men had plenty of that and to spare. Inspecting it they had noticed Sokenhoe and been struck by its enormous potential. Not for shipping out crops but for shipping in other things. Like all rich Arabs they had political connections and they had spoken to Sheikh Sayyid next day.

Whose offer had now gone up to two million. Marcos need have no direct hand in the incident – any more, the Arab had added ominously, than it was presumed he would have in a matter which he, Sheikh Sayyid, had heard was developing. There was more than one grapevine and his own was efficient. The weapons to be used in that case would presumably be AP rockets: in this other they would need to be heavier but Marcos needn't concern himself with that. His business would be to import and deliver. Two million pounds.

Marcos had accepted two million but had attached to it a single condition. The affair at which the Sheikh had hinted must be brought to a successful conclusion first.

Sheikh Sayyid had nodded agreement at once and Marcos had not been surprised that he did so. If something went badly wrong with that raid Marcos wouldn't be worth two million to anyone.

And now it hadn't gone wrong, it was safely concluded. Marcos could plan to earn his two million.

One thing was immediately clear: all depended on the line into Sokenhoe and that wasn't, as it stood, secure. Wellworthy was still free to use it and Wellworthy was an evident amateur. Sometime there'd be a muddle, a balls-up. The rockets had been brought in by a plant, the cuckoo's trick on one of Wellworthy's captains. Marcos couldn't expect to do that twice; he must get himself full control or nothing.

He laughed as he considered the means. On the box he despised it would be perfectly simple: he would hire a man to kill Harry Wellworthy. That, Marcos considered, would not be elegant and in any case was far too dangerous. He had a better plan and he thought it watertight.

It wouldn't be wise to plant again so he'd buy out Wellworthy lock stock and barrel.

8

Harry Wellworthy was in his study, the room which his wife annoyed him by calling his den. The euphoria of three days ago had vanished as fast as the winter sun had melted the snow. He had risked a larger run than usual and the proceeds had brought him ten thousand pounds. It had paid a few bills and bought that new car but had done nothing to alter his basic position. It was true that the bills were no longer spiked hopelessly like offerings to a hard-boiled editor from a writer whom he had never heard of, but his post could still depress him severely. This morning's contained a letter from his bank and another from Patricia Spence. She had been consulting with her senior colleagues and had reached a reluctant but firm decision. The only course now open to Wellworthy's was to go into voluntary liquidation. The assets wouldn't cover the debts but at least there would be a term to the latter.

He had secretly known that this was inevitable but it hadn't been in his nature to face it. He put the letter aside and opened the last. It was signed by Marcos and a scribble which he couldn't read. His stomach dropped but he read it again.

MARCOS REMOVALS

Abroad and Storage

Dear Mr. Wellworthy,

It is some time since we met and I believe it is time we did so again. Such a meeting would not be to talk of the past which I regard as behind us as I hope you do too. It is to discuss a matter of present business which could well be of advantage to us both. I feel sure you will not decline such an opportunity. If you will be kind enough to telephone to the number above I shall be at your disposal the same day.

A good letter, Wellworthy thought – professional. "I feel sure you will not decline . . ." he was sure of himself and of Wellworthy too, and though there had been no mention of urgency, "at your disposal the same day" conveyed it. But "present business". What present business? Wellworthy had only one and that was bankrupt. It was unthinkable that the project was criminal. If Marcos Scribble were still in crime the last man he'd want as partner or operator would be a man he'd despised as a petty crook.

Which left only what seemed wildly improbable, that this remover of other people's effects was somehow interested in the carcase of Wellworthy's.

Wellworthy picked up the letter from Patricia Spence, re-reading it. If it hadn't arrived by the same post as the other he would probably have ignored Marcos Scribble. The last man he wanted to meet was Marcos; he would have suspected some trap or a wish to humiliate. But Patricia Spence had put his back to the wall. There'd been three generations behind his business: he owed it to his name to accept a risk. And Maggie wouldn't take kindly to bankruptcy. The Protestant work ethic was deep in her blood. Worldly success earned no merit in heaven but was a tangible sign of a bitter God's favour.

He permitted a shrug but he telephoned Marcos. He didn't get him but a courteous secretary. Mr. Marcos was out but had expected a call. Yes, he would see Mr. Wellworthy that evening. At his home, of course, at six o'clock.

She gave the address.

Marcos too had considered carefully before inviting Harry Wellworthy to a talk. Of the numerous lessons which Marcos had learnt since he'd climbed to the top of the criminal tree, that which he regarded as sacrosanct was that it was fatal to mix the pro and the amateur. There was always some dangerous misunderstanding and so long as Harry Wellworthy was free to go on using Sokenhoe, misunderstanding or worse there would surely be. The securest way to get him out would be to shut the man's mouth with a fistful of money. God knew the poor bastard needed it badly. The priceless line of trade into Sokenhoe couldn't then be compromised by some ill-timed action by Harry Wellworthy.

It was Marcos's considered opinion that amateurs always got greedy and blew it.

He received Harry Wellworthy with a calculated formality. His house was an undistinguished one, a Victorian villa surrounded by laurels, but inside it had been modernised by a competent architect, a better decorator. Two small rooms had been joined to make Marcos's study and there he received Harry Wellworthy standing. He had decided his line and intended to stick to it. There wasn't a convincing lie as to why a remover of other people's furniture should be interested in a near-bankrupt business in bulbs so he had chosen to tell the truth and chance it. The risk appeared extremely small. Harry Wellworthy was a criminal too but small fry and therefore much more vulnerable. The last thing he'd dare to do was delate.

As for the technique of the interview Marcos had decided that too. First there would be the punch to the stomach which would cut Harry Wellworthy down to size. There'd be no playing the respectable citizen outraged by any suggestion of crime. After that some necessary sparring and finally the merciless knockdown. In prison he'd had a total ascendancy over Harry and other small-timers like him and he didn't suppose that time would have altered it. A man's character didn't change fundamentally because he'd luckily inherited a respectable business.

He had sent his only manservant with a wide commission to rummage in Lexleigh so as a maid showed Wellworthy in he said coolly: "Good evening, Harry. I hear you're now smuggling."

He could see that the blow had landed brutally. Wellworthy's face had fallen to pieces. "Sit down," Marcos said. "Take that chair by the desk."

He took his own on the other side, following up his

established advantage. "The usual things, I imagine." He didn't expect an answer and none came; he went on with the sparring, piling the points up. "Not guns by any chance?"

Wellworthy half emerged from his state of shock. "Never guns."

Marcos could smell a lie like garlic . . . So this creature had risked a gun or two. Marcos was not displeased at this knowledge since it would strengthen his hand if the worm resisted him. Customs and the police concerned were stretched to their limit in trying to stop the flood of heroin. To say that they would tolerate Wellworthy was probably an exaggeration but they'd have to wait till they'd time to deal with him. Assuming, that is, that he stuck to the small stuff. But if they knew it was anything else they would pounce at once.

Which would promptly put an end to the Sokenhoe line.

He began to talk with increasing urgency but also with increasing confidence. Wellworthy was where he wanted him, helpless. "I'm interested in weapons myself, not hand-guns but in something bigger. A year or so ago, I hear, there was an attempt to arm the coloured ghettos. That was political and was dealt with politically. There wasn't any money in it and therefore nothing in it for me. In any case criminals can always get hand-guns. What they can't yet get freely is the big stuff they increasingly need. That's where I come in. And make money."

Wellworthy was silent still and Marcos could see he was also puzzled. "Perhaps I owe you an explanation. When I came out of prison I made one vow. I would never go on a job again but I'd stay in crime and I'd make it pay. I'd provide the finance and such tools as were necessary and, if the job came off, take my share of the profits." He was tempted to add what was close to a boast. "You could call me the merchant banker of crime."

Marcos looked at Harry Wellworthy closely. He was shocked still but he was also impressed. Marcos went on conversationally.

"I spoke of tools and I need some now. Rather special

tools at that." He leant forward suddenly. "That's why I'm making an offer for your line."

"My line?" It was feeble.

"Don't play silly games with me, please. You have an established line from Belgium to Sokenhoe. I want it but not to bring in bulbs." He got up unexpectedly. "You need a drink."

Harry Wellworthy downed it in two solid swallows. He drank very little – Maggie Wellworthy hated it – and the alcohol pulled him together sharply. He thought, then asked: "You want to buy my business?"

"All of it. I know you have a place in Colchester where you store the bulbs and send out the catalogues. It's mortgaged up to the hilt so I'll sell it. I don't want your business in bulbs – I want your line. And you out of it for good and all. If we agree a price that's a term of the contract. You're never to use Sokenhoe again. For anything."

Wellworthy said carefully: "I might be interested."

You'll be interested all right, Marcos thought. I have you where I want you as I did in another life. You haven't changed.

"I'm prepared to make an offer."

"I'm listening."

"Not so fast, my friend – a few necessary questions. I have to know what I'm really buying. A smuggling line under possible suspicion is one thing. One under active surveillance would be another. Have you ever had any trouble?"

"Trouble?"

Marcos lost his dangerous temper. "Trouble, you fool. You should know about trouble. Have you ever felt anything wasn't quite right?"

"Never," Harry Wellworthy said.

It was another lie and again Marcos knew it. "I want the truth or the deal's off as we sit here."

The old dominance was still working powerfully. "There was something once. It was nothing . . ." It tailed away.

"Tell me."

"A few days ago, before the snow, I was bringing in rather more than usual so I went up the hill which looks down on Sokenhoe. A man was there with glasses, watching."

"Watching your unloading?"

"I can't be sure. He said he was watching the wild-fowl and people do."

"Did he look like a birdwatcher?"

"What do birdwatchers look like?"

Surprisingly Marcos laughed almost pleasantly. There was a spark of spirit left in this man and it would be agreeable to crush it finally. That would come at the end. Now he went on smoothly.

"Anything else about him?"

"He was black."

Marcos was surprised but said nothing. There were blacks in the police and perhaps in Customs which certainly recruited Sikhs. They were good at chivvying lesser Indians. Equally there was no good reason why a black man shouldn't watch birds as his hobby. This was something which needed investigation and he made a mental note for Demetrios. But it alone wasn't enough to wreck his plan.

"All right. So we'll get down to business."

He had considered what sum to offer carefully. To offer too much would look suspicious and too little would lead to tedious bargaining. But there was a question he had forgotten to ask.

"Are you running anything at the moment?"

"No."

"No ship at sea?"

Harry shook his head.

"No scout at Sokenhoe?"

"Nobody."

"Right. I've told you what I'm really buying – I'm buying your little arrangement at Sokenhoe. On condition that you keep totally clear of it I'll offer a hundred thousand for Wellworthy's."

"It's worth more than that."

"It's worth nothing whatever. If I didn't have a special interest you'd be very hard pressed to find a buyer."

This was true and Harry Wellworthy knew it. "I'll think it over," he said. Another faint flicker of spirit had lit in him.

Marcos extinguished it promptly and brutally. "You'll do no such thing. You'll decide here and now."

"These are very harsh terms."

"Of course they are. I hold all the cards."

This too was correct and again Harry knew it. "When do I get the money?"

"Now." Against a couple of million a hundred thousand was nothing.

"Give me a minute to think."

"Sixty seconds."

Harry used thirty; he knew he was beaten; he said with a sort of fragile dignity: "I accept your offer. I cannot do otherwise."

Marcos stood up. "The lawyers can fix up something later." He went to a cupboard and took out two briefcases. "You needn't trouble to count, my friend. In small matters I'm entirely scrupulous. Meanwhile I think you've decided wisely. But one other thing before you go. If you speak of any of this you're dead. Keep a very low profile at Lexleigh. Goodbye."

When Harry had gone Marcos settled to work. He'd kept a minder on at Sokenhoe and had fixed times to reach him in a neighbouring village. He telephoned and a voice which wasn't East Anglian answered.

"Everything in order?"

"Yessir."

"There's one thing I'd like you to check – that tower."

"I didn't know you had any use for it."

"I might." Marcos considered the comment impertinent but the minder knew his job and was necessary. He hid his irritation and went on. "I don't plan to use it but it's a fall-back position."

"You won't get me inside it again."

"As unsafe as that?"

"Very unsafe indeed, I'd say. But it isn't blowing, she should stand a bit longer." A chuckle. "But a bit nearly fell on that black man once."

"*What black man?*"

"The black man I had to scare away."

A very long pause. "I see . . . I see . . ." Finally: "Good night."

"Good night, sir."

Marcos turned to what he now knew he must do . . . A black man with binoculars. Odd. All the betting would be that he was what he'd claimed to be, an innocent, mildly lunatic birdwatcher. But a second one poking around in Sokenhoe – that was a good deal more than odd. Demetrios must check on that at once. There couldn't be many black men in Lexleigh and it was the sort of thing which Demetrios did well. He had the natural curiosity of his race and the acquired nosiness of the English manservant. Demetrios would do the job admirably.

And another which Marcos had entirely forgotten till Wellworthy's visit had brought it to mind again. In Lexleigh there lived a man called Arthur Tribe. He'd been strict with such as Marcos in prison but Marcos bore him no malice for that. He'd been doing his job, which was Prison Governor, as Marcos now did his which was backing crime. But inevitably he'd stand on the side of the law and very possibly he'd been meeting Wellworthy. To whom he had once shown grace and favour. Wellworthy was respectable now and it was probable that the two men met.

Met, Marcos thought, and therefore talked. Wellworthy had been a gabbler in prison and Wellworthy now knew enough to embarrass him.

It was a very small loose end but worth tidying. Demetrios must look into that too.

9

Marcos woke next morning uneasy. He was intelligent and paid the price of ability, swinging between exaltation and misery. This morning he was nicely balanced between the two.

It wasn't what he had done which troubled him but the manner of his doing of the deed. He had demeaned himself in the eyes of the Sheikh Sayyid, accepting a couple of million pounds as though it had been a bone to a dog. And he didn't need two million pounds, he had enough in a Swiss bank already and the money from that raid would top it up. He could buy a villa on a warm southern sea in any country which wasn't his native Cyprus. But that wasn't a necessity, he could retire as he stood if he chose to do so. Yet he'd accepted a very large sum of money from a man he had neither liked nor respected.

Certainly not respected – never. Sheikh Sayyid was a diplomat with the outrageous privileges which that profession attracted but Marcos had very quickly realised that his major interest was not diplomacy. When he'd talked in his extravagant way of the greatest political crime of the century Marcos had been unimpressed. But he had received the Sheikh with a certain sympathy . . . No, he didn't wish to know the details but if the proposition was the use of Sokenhoe that could be arranged for a fee. He had named it; they had haggled, agreed.

It was his motives which troubled him now as he faced them. Mark Hassall had once told Willy Smith that Marcos would sell his mother for money but in this he had been less than fair. Marcos had realised what Sayyid was; he was a terrorist working for greater terrorists; he had the purse of a maverick oil state behind him and behind that again a private army, men of many races, all dedicated. To Marcos "dedicated" was a pejorative word but he'd agreed to work for Sayyid. Why?

He decided that the unspoken reason was his smouldering mistrust of the English. They had bound themselves to defend his country but had cravenly sold out to the Turks. His family had had a shop in Kyrenia, doing well from the tourists and living above it. A little land too as all good Greeks should. Now both were gone and his parents penniless. He maintained them, again as a good Greek should, but he had neither forgotten nor come close to forgiveness. Well, malice was in his Mediterranean blood: there was nothing to be ashamed of in that.

But there was another motive which made him cringe for it was very unGreek and entirely despicable. Marcos had given in to a woman. He had come a long way from a shop in Kyrenia, to money and to Patricia Spence. She had intelligence and an acid wit; they had interests in common and a successful relationship. So he'd proposed marriage and she had told him to wait. Patricia for all her apparent worldliness wanted something more of him and that something was distinctly old-fashioned. She respected him for the way he lived but she wanted to admire wholeheartedly. At the moment she couldn't do that. He fell short. He was a successful but pedestrian crook and, believing the rubbish she did, she'd want more than that.

It came to him on a sudden insight. If he could show her his hand in some political outrage, bring her the Baptist's head on a charger, there wouldn't be any question of waiting.

So here he sat, the creature of terrorists. He was in the big time now but the wrong league.

And with a development which might well turn nasty.

He rang Demetrios in Lexleigh-on-Sea. His instructions to him had been deliberately wide; he had men who could handle specific jobs but they weren't as clever as Demetrios and what he wanted was less something done than the smell of anything going wrong. As the message from his minder at Sokenhoe strongly suggested had started to happen . . . One black man on a hill with fieldglasses, a second poking about in Sokenhoe at a moment a cargo was being landed. One blackbird, two blackbirds . . . No, it was too much.

Marcos had given two names to Demetrios, Harry Wellworthy and Arthur Tribe. More interesting might be a West Indian, name unknown, but probably not a local resident. Might be more interesting was now the understatement of the year.

"Anything to tell me?" Marcos asked.

"Your Wellworthy is a local bigwig. He lives in an enormous villa and has a business importing bulbs."

Marcos knew this already. "Anything else?"

"He seems to be lying unnaturally low. He hasn't been seen outside his house for days."

"I told him to keep his head down. And Tribe?"

"Tribe is a retired prison governor. He lives alone in a flat and likes it. Very regular habits and keeps a dog. He exercises it twice a day, always along the same route, the *bund*."

"The what?"

"Sorry. Anglo-Indian word. I learnt it from a girl friend. The dyke. The sea wall."

Marcos wasn't concerned with his manservant's girl friends. "And the West Indian?" He kept his voice level.

"Ah, something a bit more definite there. There is such a man and he's also a visitor. He's staying in some style at the Clarence. Name of William W. Smith."

"Mean anything to you?"

"Not a thing."

"Profession?"

"Given in the register as civil servant. Stop. Now can I come home, please? Lexleigh bores me."

"Certainly not, you've done pretty well. And I can give you rather clearer instructions. What you have is three names but no connection. If there is one I want to know at once."

97

"What do you mean by connection?"

"Contact."

"I can't watch all three."

"I don't suggest it. What you've told me that's new is that this West Indian exists. It's possible that there's nothing to him but he could be a wild card. That's bad. He's staying at the Clarence, you said? What sort of hotel is that?"

"Three star but old-fashioned. The best in this appalling dump."

"Then don't try to tail this Smith – you haven't been trained. But do your drinking in the Clarence's bar and interest yourself in this West Indian's movements. If either of the other two should happen to be seen with him I want to know at once. Understood?"

"Understood but I'm going crazy at Lexleigh."

"The sea air will do you good."

"Oh hell."

It was true Harry Tribe lived alone and liked it but he wasn't any sort of recluse and enjoyed his fellow-men in small doses. He had two books from the library, both well reviewed, but of neither had he read more than a quarter. One had turned out to be a sociological tract in the thinnest disguise of thinner fiction and the other had once been described immortally as the sort of story where nothing dares happen till the very last page of much heavy going. Where the sick undergraduate decides not to kill himself after all. Tribe looked at his paper and shook his head. The box had nothing to offer: it seldom had. So he'd go to the Clarence for a couple of drinks. It was where others of his kind did their modest drinking. He was liked there and could take his dog. She wouldn't be allowed in the bar but there was a glassed-in veranda, at this season deserted, where the bitch could sleep in warmth and comfort. Like all her breed she was good at sleeping. As he dressed he remembered Willy Smith, the West Indian who'd said he was lodged at the Clarence.

He settled his dog, hung up his coat and hat and went

to the bar. There were people he knew who asked him to join them but he declined politely and for a moment stood standing. He had noticed Willy Smith at a table for two. There was a woman with him who Tribe knew at once was his wife. At that distance he couldn't see her ring but she had the unmistakable aura of domesticity. This was a wife, not a weekend companion.

At the same moment Willy Smith saw Tribe and rose at once. He came over at his quick light stroll. "Mr. Tribe," he said, "what a pleasure to meet again."

"You've a very good memory."

"I have when I'm interested. I hope you'll join us."

"You're very kind."

Willy led the way to the table and found a third chair. "Amanda, my wife," he said. "Arthur Tribe." Tribe bowed and Amanda smiled. Willy Smith called a waiter.

Amanda was liking Tribe at sight, his air of no nonsense, no private hang-ups. Willy had told her of his previous meeting and also that Tribe was an ex-prison governor. If Willy, she was thinking now, if Willy ever went to prison, an occupational risk in the Security Executive, she hoped he'd find a governor like Tribe. He'd be extremely strict but equally fair. Not that Willy would have much chance of finding a Tribe. You couldn't rise far in the Prison Service today without subscribing to all the fashionable rubbish, rehabilitation, social re-education, the whole suspect package. Punishment was a word taboo.

Tribe was drinking his whisky and water and chatting to Amanda easily. "Your husband and I met in a curious way."

"I know. He told me."

"And I was nosey enough to check the story – about that bridlepath being closed, I mean. There's no such proposal or ever will be."

"Then what was that all about?"

Arthur Tribe accepted a second whisky ("We're staying here, you know. We're hosts.") and as he sipped it made a quick decision. He was enjoying his chat with alert new

99

faces and these people were clearly not police or Customs. In any case gossip was only gossip. He'd present it as that and play it down.

"If I had to guess I'd chance my arm and say it was something to do with smuggling. There's a tradition of it along this coast and some people think it still survives. Small stuff, of course – it always was. I'm sure they don't bring in drugs or guns but it would be different if they changed to what matters."

It would indeed, Willy thought. Hassall warned me.

And also that he himself might be watched by a Cypriot who'd been sent by Marcos. The promised photograph had not arrived but there was a man at the bar who might not be English. His back was to Willy and he was well out of earshot but the bar was backed by a strip of mirror and in it he was watching Willy. The fact that Willy had noticed him doing it supported Hassall's description that he wasn't a pro.

They chatted on till Arthur Tribe rose. "You'll be wanting your supper," he said considerately.

"Not all that badly. It's been great fun."

"I hope we meet again."

"We're always here."

The three of them walked to the door together. The man who might not be English had left his stool.

. . . I wonder what he'll do next. He's not a pro.

In the event he walked to the door behind them, not too obviously following them but close enough to hear what was said. He put on his hat and coat and Tribe took his.

"Thank you for a very nice evening."

Amanda said: "Come to supper tomorrow."

"But – "

"I know. After supper you walk your dog. We need exercise so may we come too? I'd like to see that dyke where you go."

"You're far too kind."

"Nonsense." It was Willy now. "We'll expect you at half past six for a few drinks first."

100

The man behind them said: "Excuse me, please." He went past them into the street and disappeared.

. . . Not too bad for an untrained man. Pretty smooth.

Demetrios went to the nearest call-box. In Lexleigh only one had been vandalised and that by visiting louts from Gleaville. He rang up Marcos and found him in. "I have news," he said.

"Then pass it quickly." Marcos was entertaining Patricia Spence.

"The black man called Smith has been meeting your Tribe."

"When and where?"

"At the Clarence where this Smith is staying. In the bar where you told me to do my drinking. From their manner I think they'd met before."

"Did you hear what was said?"

"At the end I did. They're meeting again tomorrow at half past six. They'll have supper at the hotel and then walk Tribe's dog. Something about a dyke where he usually does it."

"You've done well."

"Then may I come back to London?"

Marcos considered. "Anything on Wellworthy too?"

"Only what I told you before. He hasn't been seen outside the house for days."

Marcos thought again and made up his mind. Wellworthy wasn't important now and Marcos had a name to work on. Demetrios hadn't been trained for such work. "You can come back to London and your chi-chi girl friend."

"Thank you very much. I will."

Marcos returned to Patricia Spence. She was talking what he considered rubbish, the anarchist's credo in its least attractive form.

When Patricia had gone Marcos settled to think. The news he had received from Lexleigh had confirmed an already increasing suspicion. If this Smith were only a private citizen his meeting with Tribe could be coincidental but

Marcos mistrusted all coincidence and it was ominous that the man at Sokenhoe had also been coloured. It wouldn't be an extravagant guess that this William Smith was something to do with the police or Customs.

Marcos sighed. He must pass Demetrios's information to Sheikh Sayyid for what it was worth. Sayyid had the unmistakable aura of power. He might work for some Arab stateling in a position which gave him official immunity but behind him stood something much more powerful than the accident of wealth from oil. Marcos was increasingly conscious that he'd been caught up in a league where he hadn't played before. He was a highly successful orthodox criminal and to such the events at Lexleigh made little sense. But Sheikh Sayyid and what stood behind him were anything but orthodox criminals and to them they might. Marcos couldn't afford to take a chance. He'd been given a number when the Arab had called on him. Now he decided to ring it in spite of the hour.

A cross voice simply repeated the number.

"I'd like to speak to Sheikh Sayyid, please."

"Your name?"

"Just say Marcos."

"Hold."

There was a blur of background argument in a language which Marcos took to be Arabic, then Sheikh Sayyid's harsh and commanding voice. "What can I do for you?"

Marcos told him.

"What did you say this West Indian's name was?"

"William W. Smith."

"Does that mean anything?"

"Not to me."

"It wouldn't, of course." The voice had changed to something quite close to contempt. "We are interested in a William Wilberforce Smith. Very interested. He was an operator in the Security Executive. Now he is on its Board."

"I didn't know that."

Again: "You wouldn't." The contempt was now sharper, completely open, and in any other circumstances Marcos would have resented it strongly. But speaking to Sayyid the changed manner increased his new fear. He was certainly out of his class and floundering.

"What do I do now?"

"Hold this line." No. Please. "I will consult with my colleagues."

Marcos held on for a full four minutes, his private agitation growing. He had heard of the Security Executive and the last thing an orthodox criminal wanted was to step onto its secret killing ground. But all too clearly he was on it already. He had forgotten his dislike of the English; he had forgotten about Patricia Spence. He was afraid.

The receiver came alive with a click. "Now listen, since a life depends on it." Sayyid didn't say whose life but Marcos could guess. "At this moment there is a man in England who very seldom visits it. He has decided that he will meet you personally. You are very greatly honoured indeed."

"Where do I meet him?"

"Leave the talking to me. To get from this house to yours will take twenty-five minutes. In twenty-five minutes you will stand on your doorstep. A chauffeur-driven car will pick you up. A man will be in the back, alone. Get in beside him and do as he tells you. *Whatever* he tells you. You understand me?"

"I do." Marcos understood very well.

"And no tricks of any sort or kind. If this man is stopped at an airport anywhere your death will make your mother weep in her grave."

10

It hadn't occurred to Marcos to disobey and at two o'clock on a freezing morning he stood outside his house and waited. He was well wrapped-up but shivering slightly, unable to reassure himself that the spasms were solely due to the cold. Sheikh Sayyid's manner had not been friendly and the Sheikh had connections who might turn out to be less so. Between these men and the Security Executive Marcos was on ground which he hadn't foreseen.

As he looked at his watch the big Mercedes slid up and stopped. He could see there was a man in the back but he was sitting in the dark, not moving. The driver was a young Sikh in a *patka* and as Marcos went down the steps of his house the Sikh climbed out of the car and opened the door. The light did not go on as he did it but the car was under a street light and Marcos could see. It had a CD plate but today that meant nothing and even for a Mercedes looked solid. A voice from inside said: "Please get in." Marcos did so and the Sikh shut the door. The sound it made was like a steel safe closing. The driver went back to his seat and they moved away. When they had reached a speed of twenty the stranger in the dark turned on the light.

"Good evening, Mr. Marcos."

"Good evening."

"You may call me Fuchs. It is not my name."

"Good evening, Herr Fuchs."

"I am not a German. I took over an organisation in Germany but I have others and better in other countries. That in Germany was in sharp decline but I pulled it together and it now functions admirably. But it isn't my major interest by any means."

104

This was said without a hint of boastfulness. It was a recital of professional qualifications, the establishing of a new relationship. That relationship was of master and man.

Marcos looked at the man beside him curiously. For a world-class terrorist his appearance was surprisingly mild. He wore a beard but it was neat and tidy and spectacles with modest frames. He might have been a don in a provincial university and he exuded an air of almost uxorious domesticity. This man's wife, you felt, would bully him mercilessly.

There was a partition between the driver and passengers and Fuchs leant forward and wound it up. "That young Sikh is one of my men of course, but he isn't yet fully trained or battleworthy. Driving me is a part of that training. It's always possible I'll be stopped and arrested, in which case that boy will shoot it out. I'll probably be killed and so will you but that young man has been taught to take other lives with him. That's another part of his thorough training, his – forgive me – his indoctrination. If I happen to escape the shooting I have a weapon and shall take my own life. Even in England . . ."

He left it unfinished.

Fuchs leant back and offered a cigarette, lighting it with a throw-away lighter. "I don't smoke myself but not on principle. It's less harmful than *ganja* which that boy smoked a lot of before he came to us and we broke the habit. And if I seem to be talking trifles I am not. That young Sikh is illustrative of something important, a plan which went wrong because prepared insufficiently. When that Gandhi-woman cracked down on Amritsar he was one of those in the Temple but he escaped. He came to me through various intermediaries and here he is learning the basics thoroughly. One of which is proper timing. That affair in the Punjab had no hope whatever unless the Sikhs in the army had simultaneously mutinied. They didn't do so and that should have been foreseen. But one day they may which will give us an opening. We shall take it with

105

pleasure since it would suit us to see Hindustan in flames. And I do not like Indians. Their affectation of moral superiority offends me." For the first time Fuchs looked directly at Marcos. "You follow what I am trying to say?"

"The importance of timing, I'd guess."

"Correctly. I am engaged in an operation in England. You do not need to know the details and might indeed be embarrassed if you did. But you will need to know the timing to serve us."

Marcos was silent and Fuchs went on. "The essence of the agreement between us is that we have hired you to bring in what we need." The mild manner changed with a startling abruptness. "You've been paid, I suppose."

"Sheikh Sayyid paid me."

Fuchs looked at Marcos again but this time differently and Marcos could read his expression of distaste. Men who worked for cash rewards could never be part of Fuchs's tight brotherhood. But friend or merely despised accessory Marcos had burnt his boats behind him.

Fuchs reverted to his earlier urbanity but the sudden flash of steel behind it had emphasised to Marcos beside him what the donnish manner had previously obscured. He was sitting in a bullet-proof car with a driver prepared to shoot it out to the death. The man at his shoulder had more than one name but under any preferred to kill himself before enduring what he seemed to expect.

Marcos shivered again. He had thought of terrorism but he had thought in the abstract. This was real life and it frightened him badly.

Fuchs said: "So returning to timing there are things you will need to know before you act. One of the terms of the arrangement between us was that you would provide the transport to move what we bring in. You will therefore need to know when we land it." Marcos nodded and Fuchs went on smoothly. "When I know that Sheikh Sayyid will tell you but at the moment I do not know the details. What I need I have arranged to obtain but the minute and hour to do so are not in my choice. What we need isn't something

106

to steal casually from some dump. Not like the rockets you used on that bullion van. You must have made much money from that."

The distaste was now an open contempt. Marcos and others broke laws for money and naked greed and material gain was one of the engines which drove a world which this donnish little man must destroy. He didn't look like a conventional terrorist but he was as dedicated as a monk in his cell. Marcos didn't answer and Fuchs went on again.

"Meanwhile there is the question of security at Sokenhoe. The village, I understand, is deserted."

"Except for two old men and a wife. A shop on wheels visits Sokenhoe twice a week. That's all except for an occasional visitor."

"Such as that black man your minder shot at. We'll come to him a little later. Meanwhile there is something else we should do by way of discouraging curious visitors."

Fuchs took a map from his pocket and spread it. The light in the car wasn't strong and he shone a torch. He changed his spectacles and said: "There's a track into Sokenhoe which was used by that West Indian but there's a field of fire from the tower which covers it. However there's also a bridge across the creek and the ruins protect it from shooting from the tower. It's a continuation of the footpath from Lexleigh and is nowadays seldom used, if ever. Sokenhoe is a village of ghosts but that bridge is still standing and men could use it."

"The minder reports they never do."

"But they could. You oblige me to use extravagant words but a counter-attack could come over that bridge at the moment we were unloading a cargo."

"You think that probable?"

"No, I do not. Probabilities are not of great interest but the possibility exists. It must be removed."

"By destroying the bridge?"

"Not immediately – that would raise more suspicion and you'll realise that it exists already." Fuchs was controlling his irritation with difficulty. This man might be a successful criminal but in his own world he wouldn't have lasted a week. "You may leave that side to me with confidence. Just describe this car to your man at Sokenhoe and tell him that when he sees it he's not to shoot. It will be there on my business. Which concerns that bridge. You understand that?"

Marcos nodded.

Fuchs put the map away and considered; he was wondering how much he should tell this successful thief; finally he said slowly, choosing his words: "Which returns us to what is of major importance, the suspicion which already exists."

"You're sure of that?" Marcos didn't wish to accept it.

"I'm afraid I am. That West Indian wasn't in Sokenhoe sightseeing. I think you found out his name was William Smith."

"That was his name in the hotel register."

"Why not? It's a common enough name and unnecessary cover is amateurish. Which William Smith is decidedly not." A pause. "I think you've been told who he really is."

"By God I have."

Fuchs looked at Marcos with a new curiosity. Men who called on a god could be unreliable. But that was beside the point. He said: "Then you have heard of the Security Executive?"

"Yes."

"But not given it much thought, I imagine. The Executive isn't concerned with ordinary crime but political crime is its daily bread. And political crime is what we're engaged in."

Fuchs stared at Marcos's frozen face and decided that he would rub it in. "The Executive isn't as big as some others but in its way it's every bit as ruthless. I admire it since it works to my own rules. It will bend every law in the land when it has to and that means when it feels it a duty. It has an ethos, a philosophy, which is something I share but you do not. That would be an interesting discussion for a time of

108

greater leisure than this. But what matters to yourself at this moment is that the Executive would unhesitatingly kill you if they thought that that was in any way necessary. For that matter so would we if you cheated us."

Marcos asked shakily: "You think they're after me?"

"No. Or not yet. If they were you'd be a corpse in the Thames instead of sitting with me trying not to be sick."

"Then what do I do?" It was asked almost pleadingly.

"You listen to me with the care it deserves. I ask nothing of you which is out of your line. I will arrange for the bridge to be dealt with through Sayyid and I will arrange to take William Smith off your back. More importantly off my back too. The next thirty-six hours should see the crisis and during that time we cannot afford that an operator should be active in Sokenhoe. They'll send another but that will take time. I spoke of its importance before. What you do is to keep your bargain. You will collect and deliver whatever we land and you will go yourself to Sokenhoe to make sure that the operation goes smoothly."

"I don't see what I could do."

"Nor do I so don't try. But your presence there is a guarantee against the sort of action which I hope you're not contemplating." Fuchs smiled but added what Marcos had feared. "You could think of yourself as a potential hostage."

They had been driving round Regent's Park's Outer Circle and Fuchs looked through the window and then at his watch. "I have a plane to catch in an hour and a half but naturally I will take you home first."

He didn't speak again till Marcos's house. The young Sikh climbed down and opened the door. Marcos got out and stood uncertainly. Fuchs didn't offer his hand but said: "It's unlikely we shall meet again but remember that we have done so. Good fortune."

The bullet-proof car drove away as Marcos turned. He went shakily to his study and poured a drink. For a moment it steadied him but not for long. Uncontrollably he was sick on the carpet.

The man they called Fuchs drove away to Heathrow. There was an interesting little plot in Colombia. Left to themselves they would cock it up but if Fuchs could get his hands on it, inject into it his own men and their discipline, it could be turned into something really destructive. And bang in the American backyard.

But before that he had two matters outstanding. He had a solid respect for the Security Executive which wasn't as big as another which fought him but in its quieter way could be just as obstructive. He had a radio and gave succinct orders. Two missions must be completed quickly but of the two Smith's death was the more important.

At the airport he went to the washroom and shaved his beard. His face came alive as the hair came away from it. He no longer looked like a mild provincial don. He put away his spectacles which he didn't need except to read maps and checked his face in the mirror with that on his passport. The dedicated priest looked back at him, strong-featured, gaunt, entirely ruthless. But not, he liked to think, without humour.

He put his passport back in his pocket and laughed aloud. Of all the countries in a contemptible world Israel was the most detested. It never ceased to give him pleasure that he travelled on an Israeli passport. Genuine, too, though it had cost much money. Very well spent money at that – far better than a fistful of forgeries. He was wanted in half a dozen countries but the last thing a man at a desk would think of would be an eminent terrorist on an Israeli passport.

It had been a successful evening at the Clarence hotel and Willy and Amanda's guest had enjoyed it as much as they had themselves. The food at the Clarence was well cooked but dull and Amanda had had a word with the chef. By the use of a little money and much charm she had produced a well above average meal and the hotel had the sort of surprising cellar which was only to be found in towns like Lexleigh where one or two people had always been fond of

110

wine. Now they were putting on hats and coats, preparing for the promised walk along the dyke. They took the terrier from the glassed-in veranda and Willy's car to the golf club porch. It was cold with a wind, though for these parts a mild one, and the lights of the little town behind them, a glow in the sky from brassy Gleaville, gave just enough light to see their way.

Willy and Tribe had walked the dyke before but now they were going in the opposite direction, the row of substantial bathing huts left, an extension of those which the Clarence looked out on, and the golf course below the dyke to their right. Tribe who was mellow was explaining to Amanda.

"I used to play once but now I don't. I got tired of taking Sixes at Fours. In any case it's not much of a golf course. It certainly isn't the seaside links you would expect." He flashed a torch. "All that was marsh before it was drained. Golfers who come to Lexleigh bring their clubs but the sophisticated golfer doesn't come here for the golf. It doesn't make a great deal of difference if you play eighteen holes or the first hole eighteen times."

They walked to where the dyke ended at the Sokenhoe creek. Willy glanced at the opposite bank and Sokenhoe, but Sokenhoe was in total darkness. Amanda asked: "So you can't walk through to Gleaville?"

"Not now. There was a ferry once but that's been closed for years. You could get across to Sokenhoe if you walked up the bank of the creek" – he waved at it – "till you came to the other path and the footbridge. I believe it's still open. But nobody wants to go to Sokenhoe and there's no one in Sokenhoe who wants to come here. So the dyke ends at the creek and that suits me fine. No traffic. It's a splendid place to walk a dog."

They had turned and were walking back towards Lexleigh. Arthur Tribe was meandering on conversationally.

"And talking of traffic this path is a bridleway. I'm not sure what that precisely means but you can legally walk it

111

or lead a horse. Whether you could lawfully ride one I don't know. Bicycles are tolerated to the point where the huts end but after that you can walk in peace."

By now they had reached the first of them and Tribe flashed his torch for Amanda's benefit. "Rather nice, don't you think?"

They were, in fact, very nice indeed, small chalets rather than orthodox bathing huts. The dyke was strongly tapered towards the sea and on that side they were supported on piles. The gap between their doors and the path was bridged by individual gantries. "They mostly belong to local people but their owners very seldom use them. They rent them out in the season for cash."

Tribe broke off his guidebook patter suddenly, staring towards the golf course on their left. A light was moving across it steadily and as a powerful engine revved up they heard it. Tribe said incredulously: "That must be a motorbike. What does the idiot think he's doing?"

He had turned to Willy and Willy answered. "I believe there's something called Motorcycle Cross – cross-country scrambling on special machines. I dare say it's one of the buffs out practising. All those ditches on the golf course – "

"He's got a nerve."

"He'll have that all right. It's extremely dangerous."

Tribe shrugged indifferently. "It's his neck not ours."

Willy said reflectively: "Unless this dyke is also part of his circuit."

"That would be wildly illegal."

"So is driving about in the dark on private land. As a matter of interest could he get up here?"

"He might if he went to the Ninth and were skilful. The dyke falls away to the green below it but I'd say that the slope was one in two."

"Quite a challenge to a lunatic scrambler."

All of them had turned to watch the moving light. It swung suddenly left and disappeared. The noise of the engine faded, then suddenly swelled. When next they saw

112

the light it was coming towards them. The driver went through his gears, accelerating purposefully. In front of each leg was a wide metal grid.

The terrier smelt danger first. She charged the motorbike barking furiously. Willy caught the scent next and acted too. He said to Amanda: "Jump." She jumped. Tribe was standing in a frozen amazement and Willy had to push him hard. He jumped last himself as the dog reached the motorbike. The rider hadn't considered a dog and instinctively he swerved to avoid it. There was a crash as he hit a chalet at sixty, then an explosion and a sheet of flame.

The bathing hut began to burn fiercely.

Willy picked himself up on the fairway below the dyke. He went to Amanda first and helped her up. "Are you all right, love?"

"More or less. I landed where I'm designed for landing."

"Then give me a hand with Tribe."

He had clearly fallen badly and lay still. Willy felt him over carefully. "As far as I can tell there's nothing smashed. But he's badly concussed and maybe worse. Give me a hand to get him back on the pathway."

It was difficult up the steep slope but they managed. Once on the path Willy looked around. The bathing hut was by now a pyre. "No good going after that lunatic. If the impact didn't kill him outright there'll be precious little left to help." The bitch was now sitting, whining miserably. "Pick her up and try to comfort her. I think I can manage Tribe. Just about."

Willy put Tribe across his shoulder, the fireman's lift. "Lucky this happened where it did. I think I can make the car with luck but from further along this dyke I couldn't. Now Slow March, if you please, and keep it slow."

It was a long two hundred yards to the car and Willy was breathing hard when they reached it. Tribe was still unconscious, a hulk, and they had difficulty getting him in. Amanda drove back to the Clarence hotel.

113

"No night porter," Willy said, "but no matter. No point in trying to get Tribe out. You nip in and ring for an ambulance double quick. When you've done it I want to ring Hassall. Urgently."

"You don't think that was an accident?"

"I do not."

Arthur Tribe came to in what he saw was a hospital. A doctor was bending over his bed. Tribe remembered events but not very clearly; he asked a single question: "How's my dog?"

"She's unhurt and in good hands." The Pakistani smiled. A dog was to him an unclean animal but he'd been briefed on what he'd been told was an accident and his manners were those of his ancient Punjabi clan. So he said again: "Your dog's with your friends – I think they're called Smith. She'll be quite all right till you're ready to fetch her."

"When will that be?"

The doctor stuck to his brief. "Quite soon. There's nothing broken and nothing internal but you hit your head on a concrete post."

"Concussion?"

"You could call it that. As far as we can tell there's nothing worse but we'll keep you in for a day or two to make sure." He signalled to a nurse behind him who came up with a glass on a plastic tray. "Please drink that and go to sleep again."

When he woke he saw that he wasn't alone. A woman sat by his bedside silently – silently but watching him closely. When she saw he was awake she said: "I saw it in the paper so I came."

"And they let you in?" He knew it was an irrelevance but he badly needed time to think.

"Of course. I was a nurse once – remember? There's an old girl network too, you know."

His head was beginning to clear; he said: "That was really very kind indeed."

114

She ignored the cliché blandly and went on. "And you're going to need care for quite a time. I've taken a room here."

"Have you indeed?" He looked at her hard and she looked back smiling. "And after that?"

"That rather depends on you, you know. I've got quite a nice house but the area's going downhill fast. I like the look of your flat, though."

"You've been to see it?"

"Of course I have."

"You choose," he said.

"I already have."

So sometimes one did get a second chance.

Willy said to Amanda next morning: "Mark Hassall will be here by noon. After we've talked we'll give him lunch."

"You want me to lay on something special?"

"The ordinary hotel lunch will do. Mark Hassall and I have things in common but liking good food isn't notably one of them. Mark hardly looks at what he's eating."

"Then Mark is a bit of a fool."

"He isn't that or we shouldn't be here."

She knew that when Willy and Hassall had talked, Willy would tell her whatever mattered but she had something to tell Willy first. "You remember I talked about Margaret Wellworthy?"

"Harry Wellworthy's wife? I do remember."

"It's probably irrelevant – "

"Nothing that happens in Lexleigh seems to be that."

"Well, I saw her yesterday morning in the town. She looked right through me."

"That was rude."

"I don't think it was – she didn't *see* me. She looked utterly miserable. Suicidal. And you've got something on her husband . . ."

She let the sentence die and waited.

115

Willy thought for some time before he answered. "It might be significant and I'll mention it to Hassall but whatever is going on in Lexleigh has moved a very long way from Harry Wellworthy. I think he has rather dropped out of the story."

The opinion was entirely reasonable. It happened in the event to be wrong.

11

Willy Smith might have made a mistake but his wife had not. Margaret Wellworthy had indeed been miserable, staring through Amanda Smith for no reason except that she hadn't seen her. For some time she had rather more than suspected that Harry Wellworthy ran some private fiddle but it hadn't been an obvious one and it didn't seem to bring in much money. She had challenged him once but he'd laughed it aside. She hadn't pressed him and she knew she should have. He had told her his business was going downhill, something she could have guessed if he hadn't, but recently he had bought a new car. Harry Wellworthy was getting greedy. Some dubious if not too serious wickedness was slipping into full-scale crime.

To her instinct for evil was now added fear – fear of what would happen if Harry were caught. He'd go to prison again and this time it would be generally known. Besides the creed of her race she had all of its sometimes tiresome virtues. She was clean and thrifty, above all things respectable. She held her head high in Lexleigh; she was admired.

She wouldn't be that for long with a husband in gaol.

For a moment she had forgotten the manse where she'd been born; she had forgotten her private sense of failure; she was simply a respectable housewife threatened with a public disgrace. She would have to talk to Harry. That evening.

She tackled him at half past six, for at six he took the first of two drinks and by half past would be relaxed and mellow. She went to his study and dutifully knocked.

"Come in."

He was surprised to see her, since his study was sacrosanct but he got up politely and found her a chair. The

117

gesture, he was thinking regretfully, defined their strange relationship perfectly. Your wife came to your private room and knocked on the door. You invited her in and you found her a chair. You very seldom had rows or quarrels since you avoided any contentious subject like politics or the snares of religion. But she had come to your study. This must be important.

She had taken the chair and was sitting bolt upright, her hands in her lap, her head held stiffly. It wasn't a posture of feminine elegance and it increased the alarm her husband already felt. For her part she had decided her line. She lacked the arts and wiles of persuasion: it was frontal attack or it was nothing at all. She drew a deep breath before she said: "Harry, you're breaking the law."

He gave her a look which was almost of pity; he could tell that for once she had forgotten her conscience, she was simply a woman scared to breaking point. If he let her start to talk she'd talk all night but he couldn't leave her suspended in misery, he owed her the little comfort he could give.

"Listen," he said, "I've made some money. I don't think it can be touched if something goes wrong." And in England today, he was privately thinking, no prisoner's wife need beg her bread. Her worst cross would be the social workers.

She started on an indignant protest but he cut her short. "No talk. Let's take the car to Harwich and eat fish. And a bottle of wine to wash it down."

Margaret Wellworthy visibly hesitated. If she had a forgivable human weakness it was one for a bottle of good white wine. So she considered it but said reluctantly: "We can't afford it."

"I think we can, but just as you say, dear. What have you got for supper here?"

"Shepherd's pie," she said.

"You make it well."

*

118

Mark Hassall arrived precisely at noon as Amanda was still tactfully shopping. Willy met him in the hall and stared. Hassall was carrying a substantial suitcase.

"You mean to stay here?"

"Can you fix me a room?"

"At this time of the year that's no trouble at all. They'll be delighted to take what good fortune sends them."

They went to the desk and arranged it smoothly and when the porter had left Hassall's room he said: "I've changed my mind, you see – pretty thoroughly. I've something more than a policeman's hunch that the rest of the action is going to be here. All except one bit and that may be anywhere."

"Being a little cryptic, aren't you?"

"There's evidence to back the hunch."

"Then let's go to my room and talk it over. I hate serious talk in a bedroom. It doesn't seem right."

They settled in the modest sitting room and Willy said simply: "You shoot first."

"Very well, I will. This accident of yours which you don't think was one. Nor do I."

"Something to do with Marcos?"

"Emphatically no. Marcos is a successful criminal but murder is not in his usual line. Further, it was all too well organised. You could have been killed or maybe severely mangled – in either case you'd have been out of action – and the rider could have got clean away. As it is there isn't much of him left and identification is going to be difficult. But the inquest will bring in 'Misadventure'." Hassall shook his head. "Very neat."

"Too neat for Marcos?"

"I think so."

"Why?"

"Let's start at the beginning."

"That's best."

Mark Hassall collected his thoughts and began. "This all starts with a minor fiddle by Wellworthy, running in the traditional contraband, but that running was done on a

119

regular line. Then Wellworthy is tailed to Marcos's house and almost at once there's a major crime. A crime I would have you remember, please, conducted with the sort of weapons which aren't available without special arrangements. Such as stealing them from an American arsenal and running them in through a place like Sokenhoe. Which was once in Wellworthy's fief, but now is not."

"You're sure of that?"

"You were shot at, weren't you? Does that sound like Wellworthy?"

"Not very much. But please go on."

"So Marcos's minder shoots to frighten but that affair last night was attempted murder. That's more than just a difference of degree. It's a change in basic styles and it scares me." Hassall tapped on the arm of his chair in emphasis. "What happened to Wellworthy has happened to Marcos. Marcos has been taken over."

"That's a guess," Willy said.

"But a guess on the evidence."

"What evidence?"

"I was going to tell you that – please listen. You are, if I may say so, somewhat easily recognised, especially in a place like this. So a West Indian was watching birds from the Mount but could equally well have been watching Sokenhoe. That was in Wellworthy's time, not Marcos's, but Marcos will have heard of the incident. And it was a West Indian poking about in Sokenhoe. He was firmly discouraged but he wasn't shot dead."

"Why not?"

"Two West Indians were a disturbing coincidence. A dead West Indian would have attracted attention – the police all over Sokenhoe at just the wrong time. It would have been the stupidest of risks." Mark Hassall paused, then delivered the punch line. "*Until they found out who the West Indian was. When it ceased to be a risk and became a need.*"

"I'm not sure I follow that."

"It's simple. I told you Marcos had sent a man here."

"I spotted him."

120

"You would – he wasn't a pro. But he could find out your name since you haven't been hiding it, this West Indian with an interest in Sokenhoe, and no doubt he would report it to Marcos. To whom it might or might not have had meaning but if Marcos has been taken over or if he's allowing that line to be used by another, the name of a man on the Board of the Executive could be the worst news in a dangerous world."

"Which assumes that this other is a political criminal."

"If he isn't why should he try to kill you?"

"I agree he would want the Executive off his back but he wouldn't do that just by murdering *me*."

"No, but he'd be buying time."

"Which suggests that time is important."

"I'm sure of it. Whatever is brewing is frighteningly close."

Mark Hassall looked at Willy sharply. "Isn't that more your side than mine?"

"A legitimate question – yes, it is. When I left London we *had* heard a rumour. It was a rumour that Fuchs was now in London."

"Fuchs?" Hassall said.

"You heard me. Fuchs. He was sheltering in an Arab embassy and we should dearly have liked to follow that up. But anything to do with Arabs, especially this particular brand of them, is currently absurdly sensitive so we had to put it up to our masters. You can guess what the answer was. Lay off."

"You do not reassure me."

"I cannot."

"Fuchs is one of two men big enough to organise what I privately dread."

Willy looked hard at Mark Hassall in turn. So far he had been talking to persuade, almost as much to convince himself as to carry Willy Smith along with him. Now suddenly he was certain.

And really scared.

Willy said quietly: "Tell me what frightens you."

Hassall put his hands on the table. They were powerful

hands and scrupulously kept. He stared at them for ten seconds, then said: "On Saturday there's this tiresome Royal Marriage. There's a whisper that it will be attacked. By mortar fire."

"Mortars?" Willy Smith was incredulous.

"Why not? Remember it's been done before. In Ulster. The IRA had a mortar in a truck. It was a home-made affair but could clear three streets, bang into a Constabulary barracks, over the houses which stood between. As I say, it was a very poor thing and the rounds it fired were even worse. Some of them didn't explode on landing and some of them went off in the air. But one got through and hit a police canteen. If they'd had anything like a modern weapon the attack would have been an out-and-out massacre."

Willy was unconvinced but he was impressed. "We're talking of Fuchs, and Fuchs is deadly. But where is he going to get his mortars? After that affair of those rockets every arsenal or dump will be on its toes."

"But mortars won't have been withdrawn from regiments."

"But that would mean . . ." Willy shook his head; he said at length: "You must be joking."

"Are *you* prepared to joke about Fuchs?"

"He certainly has some devoted followers, suicide bombers and all the rest. But seizing mortars from other armed men would be different. It would mean a pretty large-scale shoot-out."

"Or a well-laid ambush."

"Now you're scaring me too."

"Then look at this." Hassall produced a map of London, spreading it on the table between them. "Here's the Mall – say thirty to thirty-five yards across it. Here's unarmoured carriages driving slowly, the Sovereign's Escort, the police on horses too. So one Over into Carlton House Gardens, one Short into St. James's Park, both falls of shot spotted by a man with a radio. Then wham. A modern mortar fires fifteen to the minute, maybe twenty if the crew are specialists. Three mortars would be saturation. The Mall would be a bloody shambles."

"Lobbing them over the buildings. I see. But where are they going to fire from?"

"The forty thousand dollar question." Hassall pulled out a pair of dividers, putting one point on the Mall at its centre, swinging the other round in a circle. "These dividers are set a mile and look what that setting includes. An infantry mortar fires further than that, but even with the mile I'm giving you that's an impossible slice of London to cover. It takes in part of South of the River, the warren of streets behind the Courts, Belgravia and most of Pimlico. That's mentioning the more obvious places." Hassall picked the dividers up and widened them. "They're now at a kilometer and a half." He swung them again. "Now look at that. Completely out of the question to police it. The army couldn't cover it properly, especially as on previous form whoever they are will use a lorry. Dash in and hope to dash out. They might do it."

"Road-blocks at strategic junctions? Mobile patrols prepared to shoot?"

"That we could do and maybe shall have to, but it's far too big a thing to mount on suspicion. I've spoken to the Commissioner but he wouldn't look at it without positive evidence."

Hassall was folding the map up as he spoke. He did it neatly and with an easy authority. Most men were rather clumsy with maps. They opened them carelessly without watching the creases and when it came to folding them up they made a mess. But Hassall's big hands moved fast and decisively. He was saying as he stowed the map: "I've got to get a bit of hard evidence, not just events which support a hypothesis. The only way I might possibly get it, and a very long shot it is at that, is by taking a look at Sokenhoe myself."

"Then talking of shots you may get shot at. And if you're right that it's Fuchs who now owns Sokenhoe it's going to be a shot to kill."

"My dead body might persuade the Commissioner."

"If that was a joke it wasn't a good one."

"It wasn't but I don't mean it to happen. I don't intend to go by road." Hassall fished in his briefcase and brought out a photograph. "This was taken from the helicopter just before that run which brought in the rockets. You were shot at from the Martello tower?"

"I was."

"But not on the quay where the warehouse is?"

"No, that's shielded by what's left of the buildings."

"There might be something in that warehouse."

"Unlikely."

"But still, I think, a chance worth taking, in fact the only chance I have." Hassall pointed at the photo and asked: "Is that footbridge still standing? The one which connects with the footpath along the Mount?"

"It was when I was in Sokenhoe last. Nobody ever uses it now."

"Somebody's going to use it soon."

"I'd like to come too."

"I'd be glad of your company."

12

The apparently simple decision to join Willy at Lexleigh had cost Mark Hassall a sleepless night. He hadn't needed formal permission but he knew that he would have been wise to seek it before he went. Active approval was always useful and at this moment it was close to essential. For Mark Hassall was at a personal crisis.

He was a successful officer but not everyone liked him, and there were seniors who had reservations. They were those which Amanda had once uttered to Willy: Mark Hassall could be dangerous or more accurately he wasn't quite safe; and on any ladder's higher rungs it was safety which counted most as a man climbed. Contrary to what many thought, it wasn't the simply compliant who reached the top. There were too many of those and they cancelled each other out. They stuck at Assistant Secretary, at Superintendent of Police, at Brigadier. Above them went the genuine flyers but they flew by the book, not the seat of their pants. They knew the percentage shots and they played them.

The Commissioner was the perfect example and it was the Commissioner who most mattered to Mark. His post carried with it the right to report to him and this, as he had told Willy, he had done. And the Commissioner had asked for hard evidence.

Mark who was a fair-minded man had been disappointed but in no way surprised. What else could a top official have done? If Hassall's suspicions were solidly grounded, and at the moment they were in the air, it would mean that the police of the Home Counties must be mobilised to saturate London. That couldn't be done in secrecy and if Hassall were wrong, any plot a chimera, there would be very awkward questions to whomsoever had ordered the mobilisation. Alternatively if there were a plot the news of the reinforcements would leak and the plotters might back away for another time. In which case there'd be the same questions but sharper. The Commissioner had played it safe. He had his knighthood but he enjoyed his job.

Mark Hassall didn't think like that. His father had been a yeoman farmer, far from rich, but they had all eaten well. Mark had been the last of three sons. When his father died the first would inherit but the other two must look elsewhere. That was the established tradition in a way of life which was fast disappearing. You didn't fragment as in other countries; you kept your essential holding intact. Mark's second brother had enlisted happily for there'd been Hassalls in the county's Light Infantry for as long as Hassalls had farmed on its land. By now he was a Warrant Officer and could have nursed a recruit who was also a brother. But Mark Hassall hadn't fancied the army. He had gone up to London and joined the Met.

Where the disciplines of a farming background had quickly raised him to Sergeant and then to Inspector. Thereafter he had gone forward smoothly for he was shrewd and he could run a tight ship. Only one question mark now hung over him, the suspicion that he could be bloody-minded. Well, he thought, that was what he was. You couldn't successfully farm on your own, neither a squire with outside capital nor a tenant on some frozen rent, without a streak of a dangerous independence of mind.

Mark Hassall knew that this ball and chain had been forged on him by his genes and childhood. He recognised it but he couldn't escape it. So looking at things as they stood . . .

Oh hell. In any other country but England . . . But no, he mustn't think like that. When he did so aloud he annoyed Willy Smith and when he kept silent he flayed himself uselessly. Nevertheless the taboos remained. Wellworthy had been watched from the first and Marcos was now

126

under steady surveillance. Which had yielded the fact that he'd sent Demetrios to Lexleigh; and recently, after much red tape, it had been agreed that he, Hassall, might tap his telephone. It was known that Marcos had met Sheikh Sayyid . . .

So there you were in this law-sodden country. A very dangerous thought for a policeman but with anything like adequate powers the next action would be perfectly simple. Marcos had taken over Wellworthy's so you in turn took over Marcos. You did it by sending armed men to Sokenhoe and seizing any cargo at gunpoint. No question of frightening off and going elsewhere. You let him walk into a trap and shut the door.

But of course that didn't begin to be on. There wasn't a national police force yet – another very dangerous thought – and though a force of armed police could be put together they couldn't be got to Sokenhoe secretly. Red tape and a naturally nervous Chief Constable would make such a sensible course impossible. Administrative difficulties . . .

Hell again. The Executive was shackled too, not by its inability to serve the state outside the law but by the orders it had received from its masters. Arabs might be concerned in his outrage and those masters were running scared of Arabs.

Mark Hassall grunted in quiet despair. But one thing he had firmly decided: whatever happened he was going to be there. He wouldn't be sitting at home when the heavens fell. There were people who might talk of conscience but Mark Hassall thought the word affected. He was a bloody-minded man and that was that.

There was nothing he could do effectively, nothing against determined terrorists. But he was going to be there. With Willy Smith.

The foray had needed careful timing since, though there was the last of a moon it would be hidden by heavy cloud and driving rain, and neither had walked the footpath before. Torches would attract the attention of what on the record was a competent rifleman and this time he might not shoot to discourage. They decided to start an hour before sunset which should give them thirty minutes of half light in which to make a brief reconnaissance which they had agreed should not be pressed if challenged.

They took a car to where Lexleigh ended abruptly, opening onto the Mount and its crop of rape. Here the footpath began and they started to climb it. It had been allowed to deteriorate badly and the going was hard. They were blowing when they reached the top, where Mark Hassall borrowed Willy's binoculars. To the right was the village appropriately called Breda, to the left the Mount's saddle sloping down to the golf course. Beyond that was the long dyke and the sea. There was no cover from fire from Sokenhoe and instinctively they had subdued their gestures. Nevertheless Hassall pointed and asked: "Is that the dyke where they tried to get you? I told you why I thought it significant."

"I followed that."

"So if something happens this evening too I'll be confirmed in what I already suspect." He paused to increase the emphasis and said: "Whatever the crisis will be is uncomfortably close. Fuchs wouldn't take a risk for nothing and if he takes another tonight I'll be sure."

"That's logical," Willy said.

"I'm afraid so." Hassall swung his glasses on Sokenhoe. "Pretty little place," he said.

"It was before it fell to pieces."

"I didn't mean picturesque, I meant useful. Handy for smuggling brandy and cigarettes. Handy for smuggling AP rockets. And now, if I'm right, for smuggling mortars."

"I'm not quite convinced but I'm not saying you're wrong."

"Then we'd better have a look at that warehouse. But let's have a sight of the tower before we move. It was from there that you were shot at?"

"Yes. And a pretty bold man to use it."

128

"Why?"

"Because it's a shell of rotten brickwork. There are danger notices all round it in a ring. I went close to it before the shooting and a piece of the balustrade fell near me."

"Or was pushed."

"Very possibly. But if a man can push down a piece of stonework that stonework must be as rotten as the brick. Anyway, we're not going near it."

"But until we get down to the bridge and some cover we're sitting targets to your friend with the rifle. That is, if he's there still."

"I'd guess he is. Or a regular relief. What are you going to do if he shoots?"

"I'm going to run as fast as I can."

"I shall be keeping up with you. Let's go."

They walked steadily down the slope to the bridge, aware that they were easy marks, not looking at each other's faces. It seemed a very long walk but they didn't run. Once they reached level ground by the creek the ruins of Sokenhoe made sniping impossible and Hassall wiped his hands on his handkerchief. He looked at the bridge and said: "Pretty dicey."

It must have been eighty years old at least, an old-fashioned affair of box girders and planking. Parts of the latter were clearly rotten and whole sections had fallen away from the steelwork. There was a single handrail but most of that had gone too.

"We can make it if we go carefully."

"Maybe."

They were perhaps a third of the way across when the explosion blew the bridge in two pieces. The two halves subsided gently into the creek. Mark Hassall and Willy Smith had jumped.

The charge had been blown a yard ahead of them and both were uninjured and swimming strongly. Hassall shouted at Willy urgently: "Don't put your feet down. If you do you've almost certainly had it. These tidal creeks have killed more men than Fuchs. Get stuck in the mud and you won't get out again short of men with a rope and I don't see either."

"Then what do we do?"

"Swim back to what's left of the bridge and haul ourselves out. On the Lexleigh side, I fancy."

"So do I."

The Lexleigh end of what was now half a bridge hadn't fallen when the charge had blown it in two. They pulled themselves out across the treacherous mud and once on firm ground stood shivering miserably. Finally Hassall asked: "What now?"

"We go back the way we came. And this time we run."

They went back up the Mount at a steady double. A single shot whined between them but that was all.

Once over the brow of the Mount they slowed to a trot. Hassall spoke only once, allusively. "That's two pitches across the plate and one to come."

"I think I know what you mean but save your breath. It's luck it isn't freezing yet."

"That's all we've had tonight."

"Or are going to get."

13

Willy and Hassall met next morning at ten for they had agreed that each must telephone London before either could take further action at Lexleigh. Mark Hassall was on edge and frustrated since the answer to his recent warnings had been much as he had expected and feared. His superiors weren't stupid men and they carried, without fear or self-pity, responsibilities which would have broken lesser men's backs; but they were responsible to Ministers who didn't always back them blindly and they'd been taught since they joined as raw recruits that a policeman who overstepped was a bad one.

So, yes, mining a bridge at Sokenhoe was significant, perhaps even sinister, and a Great State Occasion was uncomfortably close. Such events were a recurring nightmare to those who had to provide protection to Persons whose deaths would rock the country but there were limits to what could be done on suspicion and bridges blown up under policemen's feet didn't harden that suspicion into fact. An attack by mortar fire? Not inconceivable. After all it had been done in Ireland but with home-made weapons, maximum range three hundred yards. There would now be extra vigilance within that range – indeed it had been ordered already – but any fear of a long-range attack by real mortars rested on a single Superintendent's hunch. One couldn't saturate London with policemen on what amounted to a pricking of the thumbs.

Mark Hassall had stuck to his guns and argued. With respect it was more than a hunch: there was precedent. There'd been an attack on a van with AP rockets and the evidence very strongly suggested that they'd been brought

131

into the country through Sokenhoe. If AP rockets why not mortars?

Conceded. But where were they coming from? After that affair of the rockets every unit in Germany would be counting its cartridges. No, let Hassall produce something firm and factual and everything would be done that could be.

By which time, he had thought, it will be too late.

So Mark Hassall was in very poor humour when he met that morning with Willy Smith. What riled him, he began to explain, was to be forced onto the passive defensive . . . If only he had some positive evidence everything would be done that could be! But the action should be immediate and at this end. Sokenhoe should be crawling with gendarmes prepared to stop anything reaching London. If it weren't for laws which cossetted criminals . . .

Mark Hassall had a set piece about this too and though Willy Smith agreed with some of it he had heard it often and normally fended it off. But today Mark Hassall was tense and unhappy. It would be uncharitable to deny him catharsis. So Willy let Hassall talk on and considered him.

Clearly he was an exceptional officer who had risen to his rank on merit but it was legitimate to wonder privately at what point the door of promotion would shut on him. For the stuffier sort of senior policeman had doubts about Mark Hassall, grave ones. He held opinions which were distinctly unfashionable, such as a considered conviction that the time had come to abolish lay magistrates. Beaks had served the country splendidly in the days when their major preoccupation had been dealing with poachers on land they owned themselves. But those simple times were gone for ever. Nowadays beaks were poisoned by consciences, particularly the women beaks. Mostly they were in comfortable circumstances, their children off hand and bored by their husbands. So they went on the Bench and oozed compassion. Collectively they'd been a national disaster and many of the men were as bad. They should be displaced *en bloc* by tough stipendiaries on terms of tenure as secure as a judge's.

Hassall, by now, had worked through the abstractions and was considering what could be done at Sokenhoe. Since sane preventative action was out, what was a poor policeman to do?

He gave Willy a curious look which Willy read. Disappointment was in it and a touch of resentment. The police could do nothing since the police weren't allowed to but the Executive had more powerful tools and the Executive sat on its hands and did nothing. When it had to it ignored the law and if ever there was a time for doing so it seemed to Mark Hassall, Superintendent of Police, that the protection of Super Important Persons was the occasion above all others to act.

All this Willy sensed and he had sought action that morning but he also liked to tease and said: "You're thinking I'm a very poor partner."

"The Executive has a reputation – "

"Precisely the point. The Executive has a reputation, not your humble servant Willy Smith. Remember *you* suggested I come here – something about a holiday on which I could give you a second opinion about smuggling of the usual things which you were scared might expand into something less usual. I wasn't sent here with a brief from my betters."

"But surely enough has happened since then – "

"To invoke the Executive formally? But I have. I spoke to an elder and better this morning and we made a little plan which might work."

"For God's sake stop talking in riddles."

"I will." But Willy was enjoying his tease. "The essence of what you've just been telling me is that *your* elders and betters are still pretty sceptical. They're not convinced by the Hassall hypothesis – the mortars and all their wild boy's carry-on. So they'll play it by the book from London, stepping up security to the limits which London manpower imposes but not calling for outside reinforcements and certainly sending no men to Sokenhoe – armed men prepared to face a shoot-out. As you pointed out, they haven't got them. A handful of policemen with pistols or rifles is by no means the same as a platoon of gendarmerie. Which the Executive doesn't have either and doesn't want. But we agree that it's here at Sokenhoe that pre-emptive action has got to be taken. Your masters can't take it so I've contacted mine."

"With any success?"

"Perhaps a little. I doubt if Marcos has been taken over in the sense that he took over all of Wellworthy's; he's still operating that line himself but he's using it to serve someone much bigger. Perhaps he was tempted by a huge sum of money – if the someone much bigger is Fuchs it would be – or perhaps he had some other motive. What matters is that Marcos has got to deliver and deliver is the important word."

"Go on."

"So deliver at Sokenhoe? Yes, of course. But I'm guessing that the contract goes further than that. Marcos is in a position to *move* things and that would have counted with whoever suborned him. Your theory is that it's going to be mortars: mine is that if it's Fuchs and Marcos then Marcos has got to do more than just land them."

"You mean deliver them in London?"

"Why not? Marcos is well equipped to do so. His cover is removing furniture."

"I hadn't thought of that," Hassall said.

"Why should you? You made it perfectly clear before why you couldn't pull in Marcos and make him talk. He has too many awkward friends and connections who would raise the usual storm in a teacup unless and until you could make something stick. Which you very well knew you couldn't do. Nor can we and we don't intend to try. But we're interested in Marcos's furniture vans."

Hassall asked softly: "Effectively interested?"

"I think you could say so. If a removal van from Marcos's yard, never mind if the name's been painted out, is seen anywhere within range of Sokenhoe it simply will not reach its target." Willy added with a proper modesty: "It's the sort of thing we can do in our sleep."

"I don't enquire."

"I'd prefer you didn't."

"What happens then?"

"Our friends will have one of two choices but only two. Either they can turn their ship round, leave unloaded and call the whole thing a day, or they can unload and cache the stuff in Sokenhoe. In that tower, I shouldn't wonder."

"Dangerous. In all senses."

"What other options have they? None. Being the sort of men they are, my bet is that they won't just give up. They'll unload and hide your mortars in Sokenhoe. When we are at once on different ground. We shan't yet have proof that the cargo was mortars but with the knowledge of an unauthorised landing there are plenty of things you could do quite lawfully. Those mortars would never reach London in time."

"Time," Hassall said. "It's getting tricky. That grotesque procession is on Saturday morning. Today is Thursday. Which gives them two nights."

"Tonight, you think?"

"No, hardly tonight. To get their mortars they'll have to fight for them and that sort of thing you can't keep quiet. So far we've heard nothing whatever but I've an uncomfortable feeling we're going to. Soon."

"For the matter of that I feel the same. Is there anything more we could do this end?"

"Beyond the obvious, which is watching Sokenhoe, I don't think there's very much. But there's one thing. I'm going to have a word with Wellworthy."

"I thought he had rather dropped out of the running."

"He has, but there's still an outside chance. I don't suppose he knows a thing and certainly nothing of Fuchs or what he intends; but he might just give me a lead by accident. I haven't enough to get tough – far from it – but

135

there's nothing improper in having a chat with him. I've cleared it with the local police."

"When are you going?"

"Now."

"Good luck."

Amanda Smith had observed correctly. When Margaret Wellworthy had looked right through her she hadn't been either rude or careless; she had been deep in a private hell of her own. Yes, yes, she had tried; she had done her best. She had spoken to her husband more than once and each time he had either ignored her or changed the subject. On the last occasion he had been close to contemptuous, inviting her out to dinner with wine, then telling her she cooked shepherd's pie well. Shepherd's pie, indeed! It had been offensively irrelevant against the Furies which were tearing her apart.

She had been telling herself as she passed Amanda that she hadn't been directly concerned in her husband's crimes. For what it was worth and that wasn't much (husband and wife were a single being) she hadn't aided or abetted or even known. But to another and much more serious sin she had at the very least been accessory. For she hadn't been a very good wife, or not in the sense that that term was often used. So Harry was going to London more frequently.

Again there were perhaps excuses but they wouldn't convince her terrible Judge. It was true he had left her bed without protest but she hadn't made that bed attractive. Margaret Wellworthy was a dutiful woman and a duty wasn't something to be ducked. But she had submitted rather than happily given and the submission had not been done with grace. So Harry was slipping away to London and that would be laid at her door unforgivingly.

When Amanda had seen her, haggard and miserable, she had been on the way to the woman who did her hair. Normally she went once a month and limited the expense to a cut but today she was going to take the full treatment.

136

She watched in the mirror as the woman fussed importantly. She had never, even in girlhood, been pretty but with proper attention she could still be called handsome. She had kept a fine full figure well and her hair was still thick and its natural colour. She even accepted a modest make-up.

She tipped the girl more generously than usual and went home. There she left a message with the ancient maid. She had a headache and was going to lie down but would be joining her husband for supper as usual.

Unhappily she misplayed her big scene. A more sophisti-cated woman would have reversed the timing, seducing first and pleading afterwards. But Maggie hadn't in fact been resting; with every minute that passed she became more frightened. The demons rose behind her and spurred her on. Somehow she must save Harry Wellworthy and in saving him redeem herself.

She came down and sat on the sofa beside him. She took his hand. She hadn't done that for a good many years and he looked at her in sudden surprise. But he did not take his hand away. She made her first and final mistake. "Harry," she said, "I must talk to you. Now."

"Again?"

"I'm afraid so. Seriously."

He took his hand away and rose, pacing the still impressive drawing room. Normally when she tackled him he would fence with her and fend her off, and since she was ill-equipped with words she had never succeeded in nailing him to her point. But tonight he didn't fence, he answered back. She could see he was in a towering rage, the weak man's sudden insensate fury. There was ichor in his veins, not mild blood, and his private resentment poured out of him venomously. At one time she thought he would strike her, but he did not. He was suddenly a man she didn't know. She listened since she must and shivered.

But not with fear.

He had stopped his pacing and stood before her, for the first time that evening really noticing her . . . Jesus, she's tarted up, she means business. He wasn't without experience and he knew that though she trembled she wasn't afraid.

. . . Poor old crabby, she deserves it once.

He took her hand again and pulled her up. She stumbled against him and almost fell. He caught her and looked down at her face. Her eyes were shut, she was breathing shallowly.

. . . Christ, it's really hit her at last.

Her knees had gone and he had to help her upstairs.

He left her at a little past midnight, going to his own room and sleeping, but rose at his usual time and took her tea. He saw that she was sleeping soundly and put the tray on the table beside her bed. On it were her sleeping pills and he saw that the top was not on the bottle. He was surprised that she should need them at all since she'd been ardent as he had never known her and leaving the top off a bottle of medicine was an action as uncharacteristic of Margaret as the pagan gusto she'd just unveiled. Perhaps it was that – she had stood unveiled, and in her harsh inflexible ethos that might be sin. Harry Wellworthy grinned. He had every intention of encouraging sinfulness.

He touched her shoulder: she didn't move. He shook it and she didn't wake. Alarmed, he looked at the bottle of pills. He didn't know how many there'd been in it but now it was entirely empty.

The aging maid would be useless in crisis and he didn't trouble to wake her up. Instead he rang his doctor at home. His doctor was a friend as well and would come to an emergency fast. And he'd better arrange for an ambulance too.

He waited for a call from the hospital . . . Mrs. Wellworthy had been caught in time. He had shaved and dressed impatiently, for with luck he could catch the seven-fourteen. He was going up to London at once and he was going to have it out with Marcos.

His rage had not decreased but had been transferred. He

wasn't thinking clearly or sensibly but somehow this was all Marcos's fault. He'd sold his birthright to a hateful Cypriot, not knowing what he intended, true, but knowing that the man was a criminal. Harry Wellworthy wanted no further part in crime, not even at second or third hand. Somehow they'd manage – Maggie, his new wife, was clever. They'd sell this monstrous house for what it would fetch. That wouldn't be much but might clear the mortgage. Then they'd take a flat or a bungalow and somehow live on what was left of his patrimony. It wouldn't be enough but he would work. In a place like Lexleigh there was always work. Of a kind. There were blocks of flats which needed caretakers and rich men who would gladly pay a good gardener. All this could be done and was now worth doing.

Provided he could escape from Marcos. That was his need: escape. Escape at last. A faint voice of sanity whispered How? but was drowned in his unthinking anger.

In the train his undiminished fury changed its aim. He wasn't any longer thinking of escaping into a different world: his rage had focused clearly on Marcos. In prison he'd made his life a misery and later when it had come to business he had treated him with a bruising contempt. Harry looked from the train at the slum of west Essex. There was a cliché about the turning worm but it didn't occur to Harry Wellworthy. He had a personal score to settle and meant to. He hadn't the least idea how to do it but one miracle had happened already and if miracles were in the air Harry Wellworthy would ride them happily.

Mark Hassall reached Wellworthy's villa at noon and the ancient maid appeared at his urgent ring. At times she might be close to senile but she had spent her life in domestic service and her bearing, if not her bewildered wits, was proof against the unexpected.

. . . The name was Mark Hassall. He would like a word with Mr. Wellworthy.

Regrettably Mr. Wellworthy was out.

Had she any idea where he'd gone?

139

The maid had stared.

Mark Hassall produced his warrant card and the maid a pair of steel-rimmed spectacles. She inspected the card with care and her manner changed. She herself had no reason to fear the police and she had been taught that they should be treated with respect. Officers of police especially.

In that case, Sir, he had left a note. He had caught an early train to London but intended to return that evening.

Perhaps he could speak to Mrs. Wellworthy.

Mrs. Wellworthy had been taken to hospital.

Then might he use the telephone?

Of course.

Mark Hassall rang the local hospital and was met by what he'd expected, unhelpfulness. Finally his rank got him through to an official who was prepared to talk sensibly. Mrs. Wellworthy had taken an overdose of a barbiturate but she'd been discovered in time and treated accordingly. Her husband could not be contacted and maybe the police . . .

Hassall returned to the Clarence and Willy Smith. He briefed him and Willy looked puzzled. Hassall said: "It's lucky I kept that tail on Wellworthy. I very nearly took him off when it looked as though we'd lost interest in Wellworthy. As it is I can find out where he's gone. That's not a lot but it's better than nothing."

He returned from the telephone looking grim. "Wellworthy made straight for Marcos's house. He reached it at about half past ten and he hasn't been seen to leave it since. It is now half past one. That's a pretty long visit."

"You'll be keeping in touch?"

"I'll be ringing hourly."

On the third of his calls to London, Hassall said: "He's been in Marcos's place for a full six hours. Now what do you make of that?"

"I don't."

"When that type gets angry it acts like a fool."

14

No thought that he was acting foolishly had braked Harry Wellworthy's bitter anger. He was going to settle with Marcos finally and the fact that he knew no means to do so didn't dampen his lust for immediate battle. He took a taxi from Liverpool Street to Marcos's house.

Demetrios opened the door to his furious ring. Back from Lexleigh he had reverted to the uniform his master preferred, a white house jacket with a military collar, black trousers and rather pointed black shoes. In his trip to Lexleigh he had never met Wellworthy. This caller was a total stranger and Demetrios didn't much care for the look of him. He didn't smell of alcohol but his speech was blurred and his manner wild. Evidently he had cut himself shaving since a tuft of cotton wool still disfigured his face. Demetrios said doubtfully: "What can I do for you?"

"I want to see your master at once."

"Have you an appointment?"

"No."

"If you will wait a moment I'll go and enquire."

The more he saw of this wild man before him the less Demetrios liked his appearance and he began to shut the door as he spoke. Harry Wellworthy got his foot in it first and used his greater weight to push past. He knew where Marcos's study was and strode to it, ignoring Demetrios. Demetrios followed but didn't speak. His master could take care of himself.

Marcos was sitting at his desk with a map, measuring the distances carefully. He'd had news of the latest, essential development in the plan which he now doubted but dare not drop. With a man like Fuchs you didn't just turn your back. He had work to do, the final details to check, and the last man he wanted to see was Wellworthy. Who was now of no importance whatever. The reason for his appearance in London would no doubt emerge as the idiot talked but it could only be one of decided ill omen.

Wellworthy was talking in spurts and rushes, stammering and incoherent. Marcos couldn't follow him but he let him rage on while he thought himself. Perhaps this unexpected rising from what Marcos had considered a grave had an advantage which he hadn't seen at once. He himself must go to Sokenhoe and Fuchs had made it brutally plain that he'd be going in the role of hostage. If all went well he'd return to London but if he put a foot wrong he'd be dead or worse.

A classic ploy and well worth copying. He would take this shouting mountebank with him.

He looked past Wellworthy at Demetrios behind him. He knew that Demetrios carried a weapon but he didn't want Wellworthy dead. Far from it.

He made a gesture which his servant understood. Demetrios drew his gun by the barrel and struck at the base of Wellworthy's neck. Wellworthy fell off his chair and they picked him up. They carried him upstairs to a bedroom and there they tied him uncomfortably to the bed.

There was no secure line to the Clarence hotel and the dispatch rider had ridden fast. Over a measured mile there were cars which could lose him but threading his way through heavy traffic he was faster than anything else on wheels. He went to the Clarence and enquired for Mr. William Smith. Finding him he delivered an envelope. He took a signature and replaced his helmet; he saluted and rode back to London.

Willy read the message twice.

The mortar platoon had been singing cheerfully for they were glad to get out of their dull little garrison town. It was better than Northern Ireland, though. For one thing all women were not off limits and the meat wasn't burnt to

142

a tasteless cinder. Just the same life was often extremely boring. Quite often they went on major exercises but in these they were parts of divisions, armies, with a minimal chance of displaying their special skills. But today was going to be something they enjoyed. They were on their way to a recognised range where they would fire live rounds and have them spotted. Moreover they would do so competitively. A mortar platoon from another regiment would be using the range at the same time as themselves. They'd show those stuffy drill-sodden Guardsmen what a modern infantry mortar could really do. They could land on a blanket a mile away and intended to show those blockheads how it was done.

So they drove through the rolling countryside singing and between two wooded hills they were ambushed. An APC was leading two trucks (all exercises were operational) and a jeep with an officer brought up the rear. A mine blew the APC in the air, rocket-propelled grenades smashed the trucks and machine-gun fire swept the open jeep. One or two men had survived and run for cover. The machine-gun cut them down in savage bursts. Men came from the trees and took what they wanted. Finally they shot the wounded.

This brief and appalling recital ended with instructions to Willy Smith from his Board. Three things. The story was on the German radio and would be in the German papers by morning but in England it could be held for twenty-four hours. Secondly, he could inform Mark Hassall – of the fact of the raid on the mortars, that is, but of nothing else embarrassing to a policeman. For the Executive had met and had made its decision. Orders would follow by phone in an hour. There was still a job for Willy Smith and in urgency they must risk an open line.

Mark Hassall read the dispatch and went white but his comment was characteristically practical. "So your lot has taken over," he said.

"It looks like it."

"And so they should." It was acid but it wasn't rancorous. "What do you think they'll do?"

"First they'll ask our masters how far we can go."

"Very sensible."

Willy looked at Mark Hassall in open surprise. He had expected something entirely different, a protest against the feeble system which obliged a clear-thinking, hard-headed official to refer to some political half-bake before taking the action he knew was right. Mark Hassall was suspected of dangerous thinking. This Willy knew and had braced himself for a burst of venom. But Hassall was repeating reasonably. "Very sensible indeed, I think. They can't afford to go off at half cock and they'll want to keep the affair as quiet as they can. On the other hand the timing is now precise. Those mortars were stolen sometime today and the big event is in London tomorrow."

"Could they be got there in time to use them?"

"I think so." Mark Hassall began to reflect aloud. "That ambush won't have been deep in Germany and from any of the Rhineland towns it's roughly two hundred miles to the Belgian coast. There'll certainly be road-blocks by now but Fuchs will have thought of that and planned. That country's a web of minor roads and there won't be time or manpower to block them all. In any case there'll be no convoy: that stuff will be split in the boots of a dozen cars. Some will get through if perhaps not all of it. What does will be on the Belgian coast by tonight."

"And in Sokenhoe tomorrow?"

Hassall shrugged. Willy said doubtfully: "If they dare put to sea in weather like this." He went to the window and cautiously opened it. "It's blowing half a gale already and the forecast says there's worse to come."

"Those coastal tramps are pretty solid and their skippers are as hard as nails."

"You think they'll come?"

"We have to assume it."

Willy took up the running smoothly. "In which case there'll be a small surprise for them. I told you we'd already

144

arranged that no van from Marcos's yard should reach Sokenhoe, so when they find there's no transport to meet them they'll have one of the two choices we planned for them. Either they'll put back to sea or they'll hide their cargo and hope for another day. I would guess they'll do the latter."

"Then you're on top of the whole affair at last."

"I don't follow that."

"It would change the situation completely. And entirely in your favour. Listen. We've been thinking in terms of *preventing* something, of having to risk a shoot-out in Sokenhoe, of using the SAS or God knows what. Our masters wouldn't like that a bit, especially as it couldn't be kept quiet. But once we know there's an arms cache at Sokenhoe and that it can't be used on the occasion intended we can act at our leisure and avoid the dramatics. No soldiers shooting at foreign nationals, screaming headlines in the papers next morning. Instead an unarmed posse of policemen with maybe a Customs man to give credence. They poke about in Sokenhoe and lo! they find a load of mortar parts. And their bombs. That needn't be hidden – indeed to the contrary. There'd be self-congratulation all round. The name of the Executive won't appear – there'd be nothing to connect it with Sokenhoe. And that's the way you've always liked it. But there'll be praise for the police and of course for Customs. Alert, dependable, splendid bodies of men! So drinks all round and loud cheers for the government. A little sickening to you and me but politicians have very strong stomachs."

"I don't think it will go quite like that. The Executive likes the ends tied up firmly. And they're ringing me in an hour."

"Good hunting."

The telephone rang and Willy answered it. "Thistlethwaite," it said.

"Good evening." Willy had been at once impressed. Thistlethwaite was an experienced operator.

145

"What's the weather like your end?"

"The best part of a gale."

"That tower."

"What of it?"

"There's been a lot of talk of its falling down but we can't leave the gods to do it for us." A pause. "Oh, nothing dramatic, nothing sensational. No big bang to wake the weekenders at Gleaville or disturb the sleep of the righteous in Lexleigh. Just a gentle nudge in a convenient hurricane. Nobody will hear a thing."

"There's a minder in that tower. And he shoots."

"I know."

"Then who's going to do the job?"

"I am. But there's still one for you and here it is. The timing has got to be right to the second. Get up on that Mount and it's up to you. Radio-control, of course. A man is on his way with the gadgetry."

"I see."

"Any questions?"

"No. The very best of luck to you."

"I fancy I may need just that."

Willy returned to Mark Hassall thoughtfully. There was a soft thud on the window and Willy opened it. The curtains streamed out from the pelmet like flags. He looked down into the garden, said: "A bird, poor beastie. No weather for flying." He had to struggle to shut the window against the gale.

"And worse for crawling about on that Mount."

"What was that?"

"Elementary, my dear Watson – too easy. Where else would you have a job to do than somewhere pretty close to Sokenhoe? And since you can't stop me I'm coming too."

"A good policeman may not like what he sees."

"Then a bad policeman will be as blind as a bat. I wouldn't miss it for a million pounds."

15

Willy Smith and Mark Hassall had worked out the timing. Assuming there wasn't a major miracle and the mortars weren't caught on the road to the coast they would reach it some time on this Friday evening. Which Belgian port would be used was guesswork but it would probably not be one used before and the sailing time would be sometime at night since interception by day was a great deal easier than probing for a ship in the dark. So whatever ship from whatever port she would hardly sail before real darkness. Which at this moment was solid by six o'clock. Add eight to ten hours for the North Sea crossing according to the type of ship used and that brought you to a band of time which ran from two in the morning to four. That gave plenty of time to deliver in London provided there was transport to meet you and provided you could cross at all in a gale which was now at its furious height.

It was one o'clock as the two men started and both were dressed to survive the weather. Amanda had made them a thermos of coffee and Willy had a flask of brandy. They had agreed that the footpath might still be patrolled – it was unlikely but one minimised risks – so they'd slip through the deserted golf course and work their way up the Mount by the saddle.

As they plodded up the Mount they staggered, sometimes forced on all fours by the wilder gusts. They had decided on one of the wild-fowler's hides and fell into the first of them gratefully. The canvas screen had long since been blown away.

They waited for an hour in silence, nipping the coffee and brandy alternately. Speech in the gale was next to impossible except by shouting in the other man's ear, but by crouching below the ground you could make yourself heard. Willy pulled Hassall down and said: "Not a glimmer in Sokenhoe. None at sea."

"What did you expect? A cruise ship?"

"But she'll have to use lights to get into that creek."

"I don't think she's coming."

"I'll bet against it."

They stood up again, resuming their watch, and suddenly they saw her clearly. Her lights had gone on and they could make out her outline. Willy Smith said: "That's not a tramp."

"She's a converted coastal patrol boat and very fast. Some rich man's toy but can face any weather." Mark Hassall paused before adding grimly: "I hope she's been *fully* converted."

"Why?"

"Because if she's kept her gun and she happens to spot us we're sitting ducks to a competent layer."

"She'd need a searchlight to do that."

"She'll have one."

The CPB was turning round, inching into the creek stern first. The storm had for a moment abated, a lull before the final assault. Mark Hassall nodded.

"Excellent seamanship." He looked at his watch. "High tide was forty minutes ago and it only lasts an hour and a half. After that she'd be on the mud till the next one. Bringing her in like that gives a margin."

The CPB was alongside the wharf and unexpectedly she turned on her searchlight. The beam began to swing across the Mount.

"Down," Willy said.

They ducked together.

The searchlight went on round the compass deliberately, playing over the ruins of Sokenhoe, finally focusing on the track which led to it.

"They're looking for Marcos's van."

"It won't come."

"You're sure of that?"

148

"Care to bet?"
"No, thank you."

The driver of Marcos's furniture van was not the man who usually drove it but another provided by one of Marcos's friends. He was known to be able to hold his tongue and in any case hadn't been told the background but he had known from the generous sum being offered that the load he was picking up wasn't furniture. That hadn't disturbed his elastic conscience. He was an experienced criminal and as such had assessed the chances against him. Which hadn't seemed disproportionate to the sum which he was being paid. He had assumed, since he'd been called in at all, that what he was to pick up was unlawful but he had neither enquired nor been told precisely what it was. If he had known he would have backed off at once. Mass murder was not his line of business and terrorist attacks on Great Persons were something which he considered unprofitable.

It was a terrible night for driving and he swore. Inland the wind was less than on the coast but it was dangerous on the open stretches, and the van, solid-sided, was difficult to keep on the road. There was rain and his wipers could barely cope with it. Once or twice he had to stop.

But he pushed on dourly for the traffic was minimal. Against him there was very little, a lorry or two delayed from Harwich, and the trickle which was going his way could pass him more or less as it pleased.

He was well out of London, some miles past Chelmsford, when he noticed the big grey car behind him. He signalled it to pass but it did not. Nor did it flash its lights or sound its horn. He slowed and the car behind him slowed too.

The driver drove on, trying to work it out. It was obvious that he was being tailed. But by whom? Police would have sounded their siren and stopped him but these men were keeping station. Why?

Probably, he decided, a highjack. Somewhere there had been wrong information and the men behind were acting accordingly. They believed he was already loaded, carrying to, not fetching from.

In which case he knew very well what would happen. They would force him off the road and loot the van.

He had seen it on telly a dozen times. Sometimes the car was pushed down a mountainside, turning in the air as it fell, crashing and catching fire as it landed. When nobody got out alive. Or sometimes, when the plot required it, the attack would be made on level ground. The car would capsize or hit a tree and the hero would walk away alive.

The hero did but this driver wouldn't. In his cramped cab he'd have no chance at all.

Well, it wouldn't be down a mountainside – there wasn't a mountain to make a good picture – but there was an open stretch beyond the next village and he wasn't going to be caught on that. He'd stop in the village, jump down and run for it. There were open fields behind the houses and they wouldn't have a motive to shoot. When they got to the van they'd be disappointed, but by that time he'd be safely away.

To his astonishment they played it differently, attacking in the village itself. The grey car pulled alongside, then slightly past, crowding his offside front wheel remorselessly, forcing the reflex action to pull left. He crashed into a low brick wall, half riding it but only half. The iron fencing at its top did the rest.

A man got out of the car and walked to the canted van. He didn't look at the driver but looked hard at the front wheels. The nearside was six inches off line and the radiator was spilling water. Satisfied, the stranger approached the cab. Surprisingly he raised his cap. "Glad you're in one piece," he said.

He went back to the big grey car and it drove away.

Marcos was saying to Demetrios: "Untie him. Give me the gun as you do it. I don't think he'll try anything foolish but if he does I'll shoot to cripple. We need him alive."

Demetrios untied Harry Wellworthy. Wellworthy pulled

himself upright but fell. He was as stiff as a pitpole and weak with fear.

Marcos gestured with the gun. "Get up." They had to help him to do so. "Now come with us."

Harry Wellworthy went. They pushed him into the back of the Daimler. Demetrios got in too. Marcos drove.

Michael Thistlethwaite belied his name for he was a biggish man who thought deliberately and when first he'd been briefed he had shaken his head. There was a Martello tower near a cottage he rented. It was now the nucleus of a caravan site and inside it they had built a disco. He had been there twice so he knew the form. The walls were three feet thick all round. To blow it would take a detachment of Sappers and the bang would awaken the dead for miles.

The senior he had been talking to didn't snub him or tell him to mind his own business. Thistlethwaite's reputation was high. Quite true, he had said, and thank you kindly. But the tower at Sokenhoe *wasn't* sound. There were notices all round it saying so. There hadn't been time for photographs but the Departments concerned had been discreetly contacted. The brickwork was mostly rotten right through and there were two vertical cracks from top to bottom. A limpet or two intelligently placed would bring the whole thing down in rubble.

. . . The minder, then? He seemed an excellent shot.

Ah, that was Thistlethwaite's pigeon and nobody else's. The senior had been gently flattering. He hadn't been in the field for some years and it wasn't his business to offer advice to an operator who knew his own perfectly. But one or two points were uncomfortably clear. From where a car could be parked to the tower itself was something over a hundred yards, and the man in the tower had a sniper's rifle and had shot in discouragement once before. If Thistlethwaite raised the least suspicion he'd be dead before he got anywhere near him.

Very true.

So he mustn't raise the least suspicion. But how? Well,

the man in the tower would need food and drink and from time to time it was doubtless delivered. Thistlethwaite must be one such deliverer. The senior went to a cupboard and opened it. Inside were two fair-sized canvas haversacks.

"Provisions," he said, "except that of course they're not. They're the limpets you're going to need and some make-weight. You mustn't appear to be walking too lightly."

"You think of things."

"I do. I'm paid to."

"And who fires the limpets?"

"Willy Smith who'll be watching. That tower will come down when it suits Willy Smith. That means when the mortars are safely inside it. And anyone else who's conveniently with them."

"And the minder?"

"The minder will be dead already."

"I understand."

"I thought you might."

Thistlethwaite stopped his car and got out of it. He took the haversacks from the boot and slung them on, the straps across each shoulder, crossed. He had a torch and used it to pick his way. Not to have done so would have looked suspicious and his senior had been emphatic about that. Look wrong and you wouldn't reach that tower, far less lay the limpets and quietly slip away. And there might be some recognition signal such as flashing a Morse letter with the torch. Thistlethwaite hadn't given that because Thistlethwaite didn't know what it was. He grunted but he moved on steadily.

At the door of the tower he unslung the haversacks, putting them on the ground, one each side. He rapped on the door and stepped back a pace quickly, rocking slightly on the balls of his feet. He couldn't have raised any great suspicion or he wouldn't be alive and standing there, but he might have created some flicker of doubt and the minder was known to shoot fast and straight. He would probably carry a gun at all times. If he'd drawn before he opened to Thistlethwaite, Thistlethwaite's mission would never begin.

The door was heavy and stiff on its hinges and Thistlethwaite heard the minder grunting . . . Well, of course. Cooped up like that and quite without exercise he'd be in very poor condition indeed.

The oak door had begun to move by inches. A hinge squealed and it swung open suddenly. The minder was framed in the doorway. He hadn't yet drawn.

He was quick but Thistlethwaite fractionally quicker. He picked up the haversacks and went into the tower. He shut the door behind him carefully for the minder had had a lamp on the table.

By its light he began to work methodically. First he disposed of the minder's body. Whoever was going to visit later would certainly not complete his business if the first thing he saw was a stiff in the doorway. There was nowhere to hide a body properly, against men expecting to find one and searching, but whoever was coming would hardly do that. They'd be surprised that the minder was absent but shrug. He was a man like anyone else and had natural needs. They would speak with him later.

They'd have no later.

Thistlethwaite put the minder under the bed, pulling down a blanket to hide him. He then began on the work which mattered – locating the two great cracks and mining them. He put two limpets low down and two rather higher. He couldn't reach the top of the fissure but hadn't any need to do so. Blowing the top off the tower was not the plan.

He checked the setting of the limpets carefully – they might have been disturbed in transit – then he looked round twice and nodded, satisfied. Since the minder wouldn't be there to open it he left the fine old door ajar.

He went back to his car with a sense of frustration. He would have given much money to see the end, who was caught in the trap and how Willy Smith handled it, but his orders had been to get clear at once and Thistlethwaite, besides being expert, had been trained to obey his instructions precisely.

The ship's searchlight was still on the track to Sokenhoe but moving, probing towards the curves which masked the quay.

"They're getting jumpy," Willy said. "I can feel it."

"For that van which won't come. Well, something has."

The searchlight had centred again and held steady. Into its beam drove a single car.

"Biggish saloon. Not a station wagon. Odd."

"And getting odder. Watch and pray."

Three men had got off the converted patrol boat. Two had a trolley and started to load it. The third walked up to the car. He had a gun. The driver of the car got down. There seemed to be an altercation, then the two men walked to the trolley, the driver in front.

The searchlight followed them and Hassall refocused his glasses, said: "Something has gone very wrong. That's Marcos and I can't think why. And Marcos is in serious trouble."

"Any man with a gun in his back is in trouble."

"They were expecting a van and they didn't get it. Naturally they're not pleased with Marcos."

"Just the same they're loading that trolley. Three crates."

"And they're pushing it up the path to the tower. They *are* going to cache that stuff and come back."

It was hard going on the rain-sodden mud and Hassall and Willy watched the trolley inch forward towards the tower. They watched in a silence enforced by the gale which had risen to its final fury. For a minute, maybe two, it had been gathering the last of its strength. Now it threw it in an Olympian rage.

One of the men with the trolley had opened the old tower's door. Instantly it was blown away, the hinges torn from their grouting, the oak door spinning once, then crashing flat.

The two men with the trolley appeared to hesitate and

the man with the gun made an angry gesture. They pushed the trolley through the open door, then he followed with Marcos before him at gun-point.

Willy felt in his pocket and found what they'd sent him. It was about the size of his cigarette case but he knew that it didn't contain cigarettes. At the top was a single button.

He pressed it.

For an instant nothing happened, then the old tower came down. It fell inwards in a crumpled cone. The dust tried to rise but was whipped away. The wind brought a faint report but nothing more.

16

Willy Smith had been in London two days, slipping from meeting to meeting quietly, admiringly watching the experts muzzle it. At the art of sweeping dust under carpets London held the acknowledged masters.

The basic problem was starkly simple. A Martello tower had collapsed in a gale and under it were four men and a load of arms. As far as its collapse was concerned the tower had been dangerous and its fall was convenient; the two Departments disputing its fate could now call it a day. It hadn't held any archaeological interest and there wouldn't be any question of a dig.

But the four men buried deep in the rubble? Well, three of them were presumably terrorists whose colleagues would hardly pursue their deaths, and the ship which had brought them in had gone, slipping away as the gale had blown itself out. The fourth had been a man called Marcos and Marcos was a British criminal. But the police could handle that and no doubt would.

Willy attended the meeting which did so and again it had been coolly professional. A British citizen had disappeared and there were people who would want a reason. Very well, they would be given a good one. The man was suspected of backing a recent crime, a raid on a van which had been carrying bullion, and the net had begun to close as men had talked. So he had skipped. His mistress had been discreetly questioned and she had known he was thinking of buying a villa abroad. She had mentioned the Mediterranean but now Brazil looked much more likely. All this would be dribbled out to the Press. Detectives might even be sent to Rio, officers who had earned a quiet holiday. Mark Hassall would be one of their number.

Willy had gone back to the Executive where the full Board

was tidying up the political ends . . . The mortars themselves? Let sleeping dogs lie. There'd be a hue and cry all over Europe and the news of it would reach English papers. Let it. Outside this room, which was wholly secure, there wasn't a single reason to guess that the mortars had ever reached English soil.

Objection. This room was no doubt entirely secure but beside the four men interred at Sokenhoe two others had been present also, the driver of Marcos's car and a passenger.

Then fortune had rather favoured them there since Demetrios had acted sensibly. When a gun had gone into Marcos's ribs he had realised that he was out of his depth. He hadn't waited about to see what happened but had turned the car and run for London, dumping a shaken Wellworthy on the way. In London he had picked up his passport and taken a passing taxi to Heathrow. He was now in Cyprus and lying low. He had considerable savings there which were banked in an English bank. But of course. Being a Cypriot he wouldn't bank Greek.

No attempt would be made at extradition.

And Wellworthy? That again had been entirely straightforward. He had been interviewed by the Security Executive and a bargain had been easily struck which the Executive believed would hold. Wellworthy could return to Lexleigh and revert to his normal life as best he could. He could, that is, if he kept his mouth shut. If he didn't he'd be dead in a week.

It was the Executive's considered opinion that Harry Wellworthy would live longer than that. His wife would give him every assistance.

Which left only what was really important, the motive behind the string of events, the Great Outrage which hadn't happened but still might. But to speak of this when it wasn't demanded would be an action of inexcusable folly. Without proof it would be dismissed as a scare and if it could be shown to be possible there'd be the usual complaints that The People Had Not Been Told.

Besides one didn't alarm the eminent unnecessarily. Both of them were passing brave but one was also known to be stubborn.

Willy Smith returned to Lexleigh late. Amanda who could read him perfectly saw that he'd like to talk but for once could not. She doused her curiosity, said: "How was that Hungarian countess?"

"Hungarian countess?"

"That woman you keep in Belgravia."

"Oh, her. She wasn't too bad but you're a lot better."

"You're looking suspiciously pleased with yourself."

"To tell you the truth *they're* quite pleased with *me*. In any other profession but mine I'd have three letters after my name or a gong."

"Do you fancy a gong?"

"No, not particularly. But I'd like to go to Buck House to get it."

"You have to dress up like a clown to collect."

"It would be something to remember."

"Perhaps. Like bowling out Eton by half past twelve."

"You're a cynic," he said.

"I take life as it comes. Not like that Maggie Wellworthy who used her head instead of her blessings. How is she, by the way?"

"Recovered. She'll go back to Lexleigh and join her husband and being the woman she is they'll get by."

"You won't go after him?"

"No, he's been fixed."

"And Mark Hassall?"

"Mark will get away with it this time. I dare say there'll be some formal displeasure for exceeding his powers as he certainly did but on the file which really counts for promotion there'll be a note that he used his head and was lucky. Napoleon liked lucky Generals and in the police the same thing goes but more so."

She said on a note of the faintest irony: "So everything's in the bag?"

"Till the next time."

"Whatever this was all about do you think there'll be a repeat performance?"

"Sooner or later I think there's bound to be."

"But for the moment you seem to be sitting pretty. I'll have a bottle sent up to the sitting room straight away."

"Make it the bedroom."

"Just as you say, sir."

Arthur Tribe, back from hospital, had picked up the threads of his life composedly. The affair on the dyke had been front page material for the two local papers which lived on advertisements but outside Lexleigh had not been news. Some lunatic cross-country scrambler . . .

The Coroner's jury had found "Misadventure". They hadn't been given a reason not to.

As Tribe walked his dog past the chalet's ashes he considered that he'd been distinctly lucky to escape unharmed from a nasty accident. The days were getting longer now and as he reached the end of the dyke he saw Sokenhoe. For a week it had come to life with sightseers but there was nothing more than the transiently shocking in the heap of rubble which had once been the proud tower. Sokenhoe had gone back to its long sleep.

He returned to his flat, quietly contented. Janet Clegg had settled in very easily though the rhythm of their days was different. She was an early bird, he a lie-abed, but she hadn't tried to change his habits. It was an agreeable change to have someone to talk to and she could sit in a companionable silence too.

He looked at his watch: it was nine o'clock. By ten she would be soundly asleep. So half an hour's pleasant chat about nothing and then the rest of the evening with music. Since his tastes ran to rather marked extremes he wondered what to put on this evening. He liked the later string quartets of von Beethoven – you could never say you had really beaten them – but he also liked civilised jazz in small doses. He thought about One-Three-Nought in B Flat but his walk had left him a little tired. He put on some jazz instead, Fats Waller: *Don't let it worry you.*

Very well, he wouldn't.

Embassies didn't need formal auditing but wise diplomats put their accounts in regularly especially when they'd been spending too freely. Patricia Spence had first met Sheikh Sayyid when performing this modest office for him. She had learnt his real interest and he her philosophy.

Their business relationship allowed meeting in public and tonight they were dining out at a restaurant. Over coffee Sheikh Sayyid smiled and said: "A pity about Marcos."

"Yes." She sounded uninterested and in fact was indifferent.

"You hooked him very neatly, though."

"It wasn't hard – he was absurdly credulous. Like most Greeks he thought he was smart as six monkeys but in fact he was very easily fooled."

"So you had him where we always wanted him – of temporary use but entirely expendable."

She nodded and looked back at Sayyid. He wasn't a bad looking man provided you liked the Arab type. She might even persuade him to shave off that silly beard.

00689233

Haggard
   The martello tower.

c.1